THE MEDICINE BURNS

THE MEDICINE BURNS

ADAM KLEIN

NEW YORK / LONDON

First published 1995 by
High Risk Books/Serpent's Tail
4 Blackstock Mews, London, England N4 2BT
and 180 Varick Street, 10th Floor, New York, NY 10014

Cover and book design by Rex Ray
Typeset by Harvest Graphics
Printed in Finland by WSOY

10 9 8 7 6 5 4 3 2 1

To My Teachers: Molly Giles and Thomas Avena

Acknowledgments

My sincerest thanks to Amy Scholder who discovered and nurtured this manuscript, and to Rex Ray who encouraged me to send it. A special thanks to Ira Silverberg, and those at High Risk who enabled this book. Immeasurable thanks to Thomas Avena and William Lyon Strong who first recognized, and later published "The Medicine Burns" in *The Bastard Review*, and who fed me, encouraged and inspired me over the past few years. Thanks, also, to David Bergman for first publishing "Club Feet" in *Men On Men 5*, and later introducing me to my agent, Irene Skolnick. Special thanks to Victoria Baker whose dedicated copy-editing provided this writer with a million new things to obsess over. Thanks to The Vogelstein Foundation, The Authors League Fund, and Giorno Poetry Systems.

This book would never have been written without the love, encouragement and support of my parents. Many friends have encouraged and inspired me through the years: Jerome—for being a Saint. Jigs and Ha, Daniels, RT, John and Anti-tone—providing the center. Scott and Mitsie, Cornelius, Goddess, Schmeal, and Gary—for being there long-term. Hanna Barbaric, Jayne Mansonfield, and especially Apples—for unparalleled fierceness. The Employment Development Department in San Francisco—for finding me a job. Special thanks to my sister Maridel, MamaSo, Howard, Sean, Diane, and Darrell. Cookie Cave, Debbie Fisher—for making Iowa unforgettable. Joey—for everything. Jerry Devine—for knowing my cards. George Camilleri—for caring like no one else. David Ostrow—for a glimpse of your world. Eric Anderson—plane flights, music, and the in-depth analysis of MP. Marc Geller—photos on demand. Ggreg Taylor—for making a circus. Patrick O'Leary—an object of my affection. Special thanks, finally, to Martin Braverman—a true patron.

Contents

Club Feet

My mother and I were both born with club feet. For thirteen years she wore a cast on her left leg, and I imagine the current stiffness in her gait is what she learned from wearing the cumbersome iron. Advances in surgery, and perhaps even in the casts themselves, enabled me to overcome my deformity in only three years of my childhood. I don't remember the episodes my mother told of how I used my cast to bust open the door of my parents' bedroom, or how I loved to climb, and how I could swing that cast over any piece of furniture, always leaving a tear in the upholstery or scratches in the wood. I really don't remember it at all until I look down at my bare feet—a difference of three sizes between them. They're not handsome feet, but neither are they impaired in any way.

And I only mention the feet because no matter what other features I share in common with my mother, it is our feet, with the aberrations now corrected, that seem to express our bond most adequately. I remember rubbing calamine lotion into her arches and heels while she lay in bed watching "Redd Buttons" or "The Honeymooners." She would croon, "My son, the podiatrist."

Maybe I could have found some interest in that occupation if all the feet I encountered were as bad as hers, because I did enjoy bending back each of her clawlike toes, pulling off the dead skin from her heels, and watching the cracks fill in with calamine. But her feet were particularly ravaged, not simply because of the long years they were bound in casts, but also because she never wore a closed shoe, wearing instead Dr. Scholl's sandals during the years of her compulsive gardening.

After my first surgery, the doctors explained to my parents that I might not ever walk with grace, that dancing was just about out of the question. I'm still unsure whose determination, my mother's or my own, enables me to dance as gracefully as I do today. I suppose I'm lucky; there has always been a strong determination to conform in my family. And there is always the possibility that my dancing has really nothing to do with determination, that it was merely the improved technology around club feet that is responsible for the miracle. Maybe, as my mother would come to accuse me, it all came *too* easy, I never had to suffer the way she did.

I'm afraid I've already misrepresented her. She would claim that, in fact, she had never suffered, that thirteen years of wearing that cast on her leg (which would never share the shapeliness of the other) were survival years, not years of vanity. The stories she told of her childhood were as scarce as the food she'd had in her house. Her father committed suicide during the depression; she was born a month after they found his body on a railroad track. She was born into a family with an older sister and three older brothers. All of the children were forced to help their mother provide.

When my mother tells a story, she tells it to make a point. Her stories are used to exemplify what she considers to be a suitable response to the inevitable difficulties of life. They are like the spotlit moments when a character in the Bible converses with God or an angel. And though she is not a religious woman, the analogy is still apt: her stories always advance a moral. They are not stories that are told to engage the imagination; rather, they are used to correct what might have been imagined incorrectly.

So I am hesitant to talk about her past, to reiterate the few moments of her adolescence that she shared with me, enormously confident that her stories would not suffer by interpretation. Already I have betrayed her, but not without some justification. Betrayal, like our club feet, has also been a bond between us. I nonetheless believe that *her* stories are a part of *my* past.

But I'll begin with a story of my own: I was fifteen years old, tall and too thin, with a horrible complexion. I still hoped that I might be considered beautiful by someone besides my mother. Even my parents shared this dream, and bought me clothes that I am now sure were out of their reach. My thirst for love was a challenge undertaken by the whole family, and my mother always had the names of one young girl or another who might fulfill the task of loving me. But at fifteen I was already striking out on my own.

We were living in Miami, where my parents had moved just after my father had come back from the Korean War. He was a war photographer who kept his personal records of the carnage in old scrapbooks with rubber bands holding them closed. They bought a house in South Miami spacious enough to hide the army lockers he couldn't quite part with. These and his photographs were stored in the crawlspace with the hurricane supplies.

Their quiet residential experience wasn't mine. A flotilla escalated changes that had for years been occurring in Miami. By the time I was fifteen, my entire circle of friends was Cuban. We shared an obsession for clothes, social life, and for freedom. Throughout the city, warehouses were opened up as large dance clubs. There were always *quinces* to attend, coming-out parties for fifteen-year-old Cuban girls, staged with more daring and more money than I'd ever seen at a bar mitzvah. Once I saw a girl lowered to the stage in a spacecraft, while a group of Cuban boys danced with glow-in-the-dark stars. Even the YMHA, where my parents had taught me to swim (I was four years old when they threw me into the pool), was converted into a Cuban nightclub.

It was at one of these clubs that I met Phil Marie. I saw him drawing a car on a napkin at the bar. He wore a Batman T-shirt under a jacket. He was beautiful and I walked up to him, spoke to him. He was an artist whose concern was "the deception of the image." He was very straightforward in his work about deception; he cut styrofoam to look like stones: slate, limestone, coral even. He would cover their surfaces with glue and pour sand over the cut mold. Then he would paint the forms. They always looked like new rocks. He was tied up when I met him, waiting to speak to the owner of the bar about an installation. He was hoping to install a faux waterfall. This was going to be a challenge, he told me, as he'd never created fake water before.

I let him charm me with the sketches he penned and passed to me, evaluating each one and tucking it away in my shirt pocket. "You'd make a great illustrator," I told him, but he took offense.

"My commercial work is rocks, but my drawings and paintings are fine art," he said firmly.

He'd gotten drunk waiting for the owner to emerge out of the back room, and had gone through a stack of napkins. The bartender finally suggested he try back again the following day. Reluctantly, he turned to me and asked if I'd like to leave with him. Outside was the red Studebaker he drove. He told me he had no money except for that car. He loved that car. There were roses he'd left under the windshield wipers.

He was renting a small cottage in Coconut Grove. There was a dark path that led to it, and I remember thinking it was perfect for him, a real hideaway. He opened the screen door for me and we were on the porch under a torn, paper lantern. I remember him blindly kissing my face and tearing the buttons on my shirt, and how, blindly, I kissed him back.

When we went inside, there was only a mattress and a couple of boxes he was using as a table. "Once I get some work in this city I'll be able to set this place up," he said. "In the meantime, it's just you and me and a bed."

"I don't need anything else," I told him, but of course I did.

I started to spend all my time with him. I brought him lunches, dinners, things he needed around the house. I thought nothing at the time about taking things from my parents' storage space. When they weren't home, I'd go into the crawlspace and blow the dust off their wedding gifts. There were lamps and pots and pans still in boxes, even the stereo my sister had left when she'd gone off to college. The night I brought that over, we listened to an album I'd found up there, *Music for Lovers*, compiled by Jackie Gleason. We danced together on the porch, and in the silence between songs we could hear the lizards scrambling through the dead leaves.

Phil would stay in all day working on his paintings. I couldn't help it, to me they looked like illustrations. He took them directly from young boys' magazines. Paintings of fire trucks, sports cars, and airplanes. I'd walk in and find him with his work scattered in front of him, and he looked just like a boy himself. I was startled when he told me he was forty-one.

I would be sixteen in two weeks. When he offered to have a party at the cottage, I was thrilled by the idea. "Invite your friends," he suggested.

Three days before the party, he told me casually that of course he had no money, but that he would create something special for me. I financed the party by theft. I took liquor from my parents' bar, money from my mother's purse. I wanted all my friends to see how he'd gone all-out for me. There were cheese spreads, crackers, breads, wine, pâté. I took a string of lights from my parents' storage and hung them from the trees in the yard. By the time the guests began to arrive, I was exhausted.

Phil did all the entertaining. He made sure glasses were full. It didn't matter that he never bothered to refill my glass. I wasn't a guest. I was certainly independent enough to pour my own drinks.

The party seemed to be going on without me, and I was drunk enough to consider the possibility that may have been happening all the time. No one seemed to notice when I lay down on the grass and fell asleep.

When I woke up, the lights I'd strung in the trees were turned off. The party had dispersed. I staggered up to the cottage and let myself in. Phil was naked on the bed with my friend, Raul. They had a candle burning and the *Music for Lovers* record playing on the stolen stereo. I'd hoped for the comic moment when they'd both scramble for clothes, or tell me I was drunk and misinterpreting what I was seeing. But neither of them moved, except to turn and look at me, as though I was a maid who hadn't noticed the "Do Not Disturb" sign.

I guess I thought, if they're not going to be the spectacle, I'll just have to do that, too. I started to grab everything I'd stolen and brought to Phil. I pulled out the stereo and gathered up the bedside lamp, blankets, and chairs. And when it dawned on me that I could never carry it out of there, I left it all in the corner of the room like a surrogate me, an imposing totem of my generosity and their indebtedness.

When I lost my patience with Phil, I lost it for my parents and home life as well. It wasn't innocence, but some kind of faith that I'd lost. I let my parents know I was miserable, but I kept my reasons from them. I told my friends the whole story, except the parts about my stealing all that stuff. I guess I didn't trust them with that blackmail material. No doubt, my mother would have trusted any source who claimed to know the truth about her fine china, missing then for at least a week.

My mother proffered comfort with one of her own stories, and I believe it was told with a number of intents, some of which she was unaware of. In retrospect, it seems her sharing this story was the way she tried to induce me to share mine. But I think she was skeptical that it would work, and so her story, by the end of her telling it, became something of a parable on the self-indulgence of suffering.

She began by claiming that she never felt pretty or desired by anyone. She was fifteen, and the cast on her leg had become more of a cage in which she lived.

It was her older sister, Evie, who first began to adorn herself with makeup and jewelry, and whose figure could make the plain dresses she wore receive undue attention. They were living in New York during World War II, and though men in uniform were a common sight, my mother thought of them all as young heroes, and she described a line of white-suited sailors with their perfect black shoes standing along the piers like a contingent of angels. She and Evie walked past them with a bag of groceries they were bringing home; the men circled around Evie and took the bag from her hands, and with her burden lifted, they coaxed her down to the beach.

Three of the sailors, the most handsome of them, wanted to walk with Evie along the shore. My mother, with her iron cast, could barely manage to walk across the sand. Evie asked her to stand by the rocks. The sailor with the grocery bag placed it down beside her and told my mother to keep her eye on it, then winked at her before he ran off to join the others at the surf.

She watched them disappear under the piers, and it was a long while before they returned. I can't imagine what she thought about while they were gone, perhaps that they had taken her sister to heaven. But when they returned, more than an hour later, she was still standing where they'd left her. There was sand on the mens' uniforms and in her sister's hair. After trudging up the beach, one sailor had his arm around Evie's shoulder, his fingers dangerously close to her breast.

Before the sailor gathered up the sack of groceries to carry back to the house, he made an attempt to lift my mother up and spin her around. But while my mother had stood in the sun, the cast had grown searing hot, and when the sailor touched it, it scalded his hand. The others laughed as he clutched his hand between his legs, cursing and whining.

That same year, Evie got pregnant and disclosed to my mother that she wasn't sure who the father was. If it was the man she suspected it was, he was probably at sea. They went to my grandmother who found someone to perform the abortion. Evie hemorrhaged; she eventually healed, but could not have children.

My mother's embarrassment and suffering was temporary, like a hand withdrawn from a flame. But Evie's misery was like a cast for life, and made my mother's cast seem a small inconvenience. In fact, my mother claimed her cast had protected her from devils disguised as angels.

I don't claim to have told the story the way she did. She was much more frugal with words. But I've told it the way I remembered it. I remember it as a story she benefited from by telling, and that is what makes me doubt she ever told it truthfully.

At the time, I certainly doubted that all misfortune has its benefits. I didn't think that my friend, Raul, might also be betrayed by my lover, and that would somehow compensate for my humiliation. I doubted, also, that every story deserves another story. My mother sat back with her arms folded across her stomach and waited. When she discovered my story was not forthcoming, she finally asked me why I had become so morbid. That was the term she used, not *depressed*, which was a word she would not fathom. That was a word for shrinks and people who depended on them.

I don't think it was in the spirit of rebellion that I concealed it from her. I believed then, as I do now, that some stories are our own, and that by telling them too soon, we limit their effect on us. I admit, I wanted to experience the full, protracted suffering I associated with the loss of a lover. I was also sure that my mother was not interested in understanding, but in remedying my problem. We sat at a deadlock; she urging my divulgence, me denying her, until she became exasperated and went in to bed.

My mother once said, "A mother knows everything." She meant for me to understand that as her responsibility. I'll tell you how I luridly imagined what happened as a result of this precept: frustrated by my silence, she must have lain awake long after my father had fallen asleep, and some inkling of intuition or suspicion led her to believe that I possessed something that would answer her questions.

She waited until I left the house before she began a thorough cleaning of my room. She found what she was looking for in my dresser, but she must have turned over several pungent jockstraps, none of which were mine (at the time I had weekend employment at a Jewish country club where I was as able a locker-room attendant as my mother was a housecleaner). I'm still disturbed today by her oversight. Had she recognized the use I made of those jocks, she might have been embarrassed from further inquiry. But rummaging further, she found the letter, and it was the letter that enabled her to launch her inquisition without having to imagine a thing.

She was setting the table for a game of mahjong. Her friends would be arriving in a couple of hours. She was filling ceramic bowls with candy and nuts. When I arrived home, she looked up as though she was startled, and perhaps she was; I'm sure she could not help but to have seen me differently.

But I saw something had changed in her, too. It was a look of shame that had irrepressibly risen to her surface. It was the shame she had denied by her storytelling.

"Do you want to tell me something?" she asked finally.

She came around the table and squeezed my arm. "You don't need to tell me. I'm already well aware," she said, and pulled the letter from an apron pocket.

I could easily re-create the argument that ensued, with both of us playing defensively, because arguments around the issue of privacy have never ceased for me, nor have the strategies changed. What I found most compelling was my mother's insistence that one must "fit in," that if I chose the life of a homosexual I would be ostracized, singled out, kept apart.

And I imagined myself sitting alone on a beach somewhere, sharing my mother's unvoiced humiliation while a muscle-bound cartoon kicked sand in my face. I said to her, "Perhaps I will have to learn about devils disguised as angels."

Curfews were instituted in the belief that homosexuality existed only when practiced. These were desperate measures that I couldn't be bound by, and I remember pulling up in a car full of friends as the sun rose. My mother would be preparing my breakfast and about to wake me when I would come in the front door, just ready to fall asleep. There were the tedious arguments that never broadened our understanding of each other. And then grudging silences.

You may wonder what my father's reaction was to all this. His was an imposing presence wearing massive suits from Big and Tall shops, but beneath the mafia looks and dark glasses he was really terrified by conflict. He wept when my mother showed him the letter, but refused her suggestion that he have a little talk with me. He was a traveling salesman and I never saw much of him but one day the phone rang. "How are you, Dad?" I asked. His voice was shaky and finally broke on the other end. He asked to speak to my mother. I remember sitting in the kitchen while she spoke to him on the phone.

"You did what?" I heard her asking. "What are we going to do now?" And finally I heard her say, "Then make an appointment with a psychiatrist and explain to your boss that you can still work while you see him."

"Your father's had a nervous breakdown," she said. "He walked out of a store with the equipment he'd just sold them. They found him placing the cameras in his trunk."

His boss had already suspended him from further work until he was fully evaluated by a psychiatrist. I think we all sensed that there was no specific amount of time implied by this. My father never did resume work for that company.

Not that he didn't conform to the wishes of his boss—he did seek out the counsel of a psychiatrist, and after each session defended himself against my mother's ire. For her, the whole thing was an embarrassment; I believe she felt that there was an analogy between a twisted mind and a twisted limb, and that a therapy should be first and foremost corrective.

"And what did you discover today?" she would ask him.

"How much longer?"

And despite the fact that my father grew sullen and timid in response to these questions, his withdrawal and vagueness only assured her that his sessions were not working. It was only a month before she demanded his return to work. I heard them talking about it late one night after I had arrived home, silently unlocking the door, taking off my shoes, and drifting past their bedroom. I heard him sobbing, and stopped to listen.

"What can I say to Epstein?" I heard him ask. "I have nothing conclusive to bring him."

"Use that," she said. "Tell him the therapy isn't working. Explain to him what was on your mind when you did it, not in detail, but tell him that your son is having problems and that you collapsed under the stress."

Their voices lowered and I could no longer hear them, even with my ear pressed to the door, but my mind was full of talk, and I urged myself to believe that I wasn't at the root of my father's collapse. For the first time I began to pity my father, fearing that he would lose the one opportunity he had to understand the real source of his anxiety. But I could not trust my pity, fearing that my mother may have clarified his problem in the defining terms that are characteristic of her stories.

I slept fretfully and was up when they awoke the next morning. My mother laid out the clothes my father was to wear to his interview. He smiled at me, pitifully, from their bedroom doorway, then closed the door before he began putting on the prescribed suit. My mother was busy cutting grapefruits in the kitchen, and sprinkling sugar on each half.

I sat with them at the breakfast table. My mother tucked a bib over my father's shirt and tie. She complimented his barber who had trimmed his hair just a few days before. After he had eaten his grapefruit and stood away from the table, she came up close to him and straightened his tie and held out the jacket for him to slip on. I hadn't seen that doting tenderness in years, and I felt strangely moved and terrified at the same time.

She came back to the table to clear away our dishes and her mood had already darkened. I waited to see if she would mention the interview, but she did not. Instead, she began talking about the neighbors whose homes she'd watch through the mirrored window in the living room. I already recognized that her stories about the neighbors were her roundabout way of confronting me. She asked me about the good-for-nothing son of Mrs. Rosenbloom, who was growing pot plants along the side of their house. She'd watch his comings and goings with keen interest.

Finally she said, "The days of entertaining our neighbors are long gone. Every time Ruth speaks to me she wants to know about your father and you; she acts as though we're some kind of TV show—there for her entertainment."

For as long as I could remember, Ruth Rosenbloom had been the bane of my mother's existence. She'd once told me about the horrible affront Ruth had committed on the day of my bris. At the time, my parents had been friendly with the neighbors. They had just moved into their home. There are photographs of my parents entertaining the neighbors on the lawn, all of them with drinks in their hands and a grill smoking in the background. The neighbors had returned these gestures by helping with house repairs, and throughout my mother's pregnancy they had urged her to take a less active role in the construction of a fence around their property. It was only in the middle of her eighth month that my mother could be convinced to put down her hammer and take on the role of supervisor. She remains proud of the fact that she saw the fence completed in her first two hours of labor pains; it was only then that she allowed my father to rush her to the hospital, with the neighbors in a caravan behind.

She claims that I was born without hesitancy, which surprises me even to this day. But then, my birth has been so mythologized by her, it seems more likely that this "anxiousness to enter the world" was merely a response to my early complaints at having been born at all. She has admitted, however, that I was an ugly baby, and that it was with horror that she recognized my turned feet.

The neighbors gathered outside the glass window to watch me, while my mother wept to my father that she was responsible for my deformity.

She remained inconsolable until my father sought a doctor's intervention. He assured her of the commonness of my condition, and that modern medicine had led us away from the primitive measures she had endured as a child, and though he doubted I would dance, he consoled her that my childhood would be normal and happy. His authority soothed her, and she was soon able to accept the congratulations from the neighbors who filed in around her bedside.

So, of course, by the time of my circumcision, my neighbors were all fully aware of the fact that I was a child awaiting two surgeries, my penis and later my foot, and certainly they knew that I would wear a cast on my foot long before I wore a pair of baby shoes. And that is how Ruth made her grave mistake. She brought to the bris, as a gift, a pair of plain, white baby shoes.

Did this gift signify her hope for the future when my feet would no longer turn away from each other? My mother chose not to believe so, and from that point forward, she kept a firm distance from Ruth, and almost all the neighbors, as though they each possessed the same potential for ignorant or intentional malice, which she equated.

Her isolationism might have worked while I was younger, but while my father was unemployed and I was climbing out of my window in the middle of the night, my mother was certain the neighbors were collecting the information, waiting to humiliate her yet again. She suddenly had both of us to attend to, which took some of her attention off me and enabled me to resume a private life which had been prematurely and far too brightly illuminated. After all, I was no more rebellious than my peers, just more committed.

I discovered a drag club on Miami Beach which flaunted its tacky exoticism. The performers were either overweight or anorexic and desperately untalented. But I could watch them for hours, one after the other making a show of their failures, their alcoholism, and their bad attitudes. One could expect the bouncers to have to remove Lola from the stage; her numbers had the tendency to become an assault on the audience, baiting them to get up on stage and do a better job than she if they thought they could. And she would only leave the stage when the bartender or someone in the audience promised to buy her a drink.

I marveled at how they lived. As much as I doubted my parents' values, I assumed that at some point I would be forced to share them. It was these amateur drag shows that made me realize just how vast the world was. The drag queens challenged everything, not simply gender, but propriety as well. If they sensed they were being laughed at, they laughed along before the joke got too old.

I planned a party for a weekend when my parents were leaving town. It was my mother's prescription of a "rest cure" for my father. Though many of the guests had attended my birthday party at the cottage, the spirit of this party was radically different. I chose my parents' bedroom to act as an orgy room, replacing their reading lights with red bulbs. I moved the stereo from my bedroom into the living room and cleared the shelves of my mother's kewpie collection and my father's Norman Rockwell ingots. I invited the guests to come in drag, to bring drugs and alcohol, and to bring pajamas if they wanted to sleep over.

I remember being tentative about the music and the noise, but my friends' assurances overrode my concerns, at least temporarily. A once smoke-free environment had my eyes watering in just a few hours. Before I knew it, friends had invaded my parents' bar and medicine cabinet, traipsing around drunk and on Valiums, dressing each other up and undressing each other in every corner of every room. I wandered around like a good hostess in one of my mother's aprons, offering cocktails to the guests and urging couples in various states of undress to use my parents' bedroom for the unholy acts.

Things died down by the early morning. Many of the guests had gone home; some were sleeping on the couches and floor. I found myself cleaning up bottles and overturned ashtrays, stray articles of clothing, and even some of my mother's makeup that someone had drawn from her bag in the bathroom. I was suddenly engulfed with anxiety, with fantasies of them arriving home early, and with the facts of the bottles missing from their bar, their bedding wet with semen and spilled champagne, and the smoke which seemed to linger even with the windows and doors open.

A friend of mine, Armando, held the trash bag open as we moved among the bodies. For each of my worries he offered tender assurances, and when the last bottle had been picked up, he led me toward my bedroom and urged me to sleep with him. When we turned on the bedroom light, some moans issued up from beneath the blankets.

"Let's try your parents' bed," he suggested. He took off his clothes and crawled over the filthy sheets. I joined him, naked, on their bed. There was a tremendous erotic charge in my final act of defilement. Our mouths and our chests came together, and I felt my feet digging into the velour spread piled at the foot of their bed. I looked into the eyes of the framed photograph of my mother; at the bottom of it she inscribed her dedication to my father and I whispered it in Armando's ear, " 'All my love to you, Baby.' "

I'd never walked in on my parents having sex, nor had I heard them. Sometimes I would find them in the morning asleep with the television still on and a pizza box with some leftover slices between them. My father expressed his affection through telling dirty jokes which my mother would respond to with feigned shock even though she would often have to remind him of the punch line. Having sex in their bed was not exciting because of any of their activity. If anything, I felt I was originating the primal scene, and my excitement was generated by the idea of them walking in on me.

It is assuredly this erotic fixation with being discovered that prevented my housecleaning of the following day from perfectly masking the events of the night before. Certainly, I'd come close. I mopped and dusted, put everything back where it belonged, washed sheets and towels, and even went so far as to replace some of the bottles of alcohol in the bar. The rest, I had hoped, would go unnoticed.

What I'd neglected, of course, was the makeup. Nothing was mentioned, however, until my father returned from his interview with Epstein, visibly distraught as though he himself had been caught in some perverse act. He stood for a moment unsure in the doorway. If my mother hadn't been so quick to greet him, I suspect he would have quietly turned and fled.

"How did it go?" she demanded, her hands on her waist, as though she was defending something behind her.

"They've asked me not to come back," he said quietly. Then, in a moment I wish I hadn't observed, he looked at her tearfully and asked her, "Do you want me to leave?"

Even my mother looked awkward, her mouth searching out an expression comforting but firm.

"Come in," she said.

I snuck back into my bedroom while they talked in the kitchen. Though I didn't want to hear them, I couldn't bring myself to drown them out completely with my records. I cannot claim surprise at hearing my name spoken in the exasperated and angry tone that by now seemed inherent in the name itself. It had been two weeks since the party and I had, to some extent, been waiting to be invoked. The fact that it was an unrelated matter, my father's unaccountable theft and its repercussions, did not surprise me either. By that time, it was impossible to localize a problem or blame. Nothing any of us did was discrete anymore.

I went to the record player and shut it off; I'd come to the last disc of Berg's *Lulu* and worried that its cacophonous climax might fuel their accusations of me. My mother had come a long way in her assessment of my antisocial behavior: where I'd once been the flawed product of their conscientious upbringing, I now had taken on the dramatic proportions of a stranger, a boarder at whose mercy they found themselves.

I overheard her assurances to my father that he was not to blame, he was not mad. I needed help. If they continued to allow me to go on the way that I was going, the family (and this she pronounced like a curse) would rot from within. Perhaps my new position as a sort of stranger within the family made my parents naturally superstitious of me. It was this superstition that had suddenly driven my mother to believe in something she had never had faith in before: psychiatry.

True, she had gone along with my father's recommended therapy but the fact that it had failed to produce results for him supports my opinion that it was a leap of faith, the calling in of the witch doctor or exorcist, that my mother resorted to while scheduling an appointment for me. I was summoned to the kitchen where she offered me the time and date from a Post-It stuck to the tip of her finger. In another clinical gesture, she dangled her makeup bag before me and asked, "Do you want to tell me about this?"

"No," I answered, as there really was nothing to tell. Had she taken the jockstraps from my drawer, I might have blushed. She had, in this case, allowed her imagination to fill in the gaps. The missing makeup and apparent return of some gouged and mutilated lipsticks and eyeshadows were the basis for her assumption that I had gone on to the next step of homosexual development: the inevitable renunciation of my gender. This theory went along with another of her theories, that using her makeup was an attempt on my part to mimic a heterosexual lifestyle. I'm still unsure as to whether she considered that hopeful.

As ludicrous as the accusations were, any attempt at refuting them on my part were viewed as understandable lies in the face of such shameful behavior. And so I tempered my responses, which were initially quite negative, and consented to their suggestion that I see the psychiatrist. After all, what could it hurt? I reminded myself that it was my mother, and not I, who had such doubts about them.

One thing I was certain of was that my mother and I had gone as far as we could talking with each other. Everything we said seemed to have some other meaning beneath it, and in the same way that my mother walks with that stiffness from so many years in casts, I seem to maintain an inhibition in my language, finding in it an inherent, or possibly inherited, quality of concealment.

I didn't believe that it was communication we were both attempting. It has taken this much time to recognize that we did not so much want to discover each other's secrets, but to find a way to reveal ourselves. I am sure now that we were both trapped in one of the great and painful deceits of language: the promise of its transparency. It was this dream of nakedness that drove my mother to the most drastic, literal acts.

I began seeing the psychiatrist, a middle-aged Jewish woman with whom I felt immediately at home. And it was in her office, with its dark wood and draperies, its shelf of leather-bound books including the complete standard edition of Freud's works, that I began to understand the significance of our club feet.

I was withdrawn from therapy at the crucial junction when the conflict with my mother seemed best handled with her at one of the sessions. The therapist had asked both my parents to come to the session so as not to put my mother on the defensive. But from the moment I broached the news to them that Miriam and I felt we could accomplish a great deal if they would join me for just one session, my mother began to fear a setup.

"Why should I go?" she asked. "It's your problem."

Well, at one point it was my problem, then it was my father's problem, and now it's the witch doctor's problem, I thought. Anyway, with much resistance, she and my father drove me to her office and decided they would come in for a short while.

Before my mother sat down, she asked, "Have you made any progress with him?"

It was the first time that I saw my therapist caught off guard, but I had warned her. She urged them to sit down, and took a seat herself. She regained her composure then, asking my mother, in a volley, what kind of progress she had expected.

While my mother turned uncomfortably in her chair, Miriam began speaking verbatim, as though a copy of Freud's famous letter to the mother of a homosexual son had been freshly drawn from its envelope. All the great lines were there, " 'It cannot be classified as an illness...a variation of the sexual function…many highly respected individuals of ancient and modern times…' " But her most impressive performance came when, quoting Freud, she directed his appeal to my mother as though they were her words. " 'By asking me if I can help you, you mean, I suppose, if I can abolish homosexuality and make normal heterosexuality take its place…' " She shook her head, sadly explaining that my sexual preference was not the source of my conflicts. "It is the family—" she began to assert.

My mother was enraged. "You want to tell me what's normal?" she asked, her voice painfully restrained. "I suppose you regard it as normal the fact that he dresses like a woman? That he steals his father's underwear?"

I turned to watch my father as he drew a handkerchief from his pocket and wiped his eyes under his glasses. He reached out and took my mother's arm. "Let's go, honey," he said sniffling.

She pulled away from him as though she was disgusted with everyone in the room.

"And what kind of role model do you think you are?" she asked my father scornfully. "Sitting there crying. You've never had a moment of strength in your life."

"That's not fair," I interjected.

She gathered her purse and coat and stood up.

"What's not fair?" she asked. "All I wanted was for you to have a chance at a normal life. They'll never accept you. It's like you've chosen to be deformed. Why would anyone choose that for themselves?" I wanted to answer her, but she and my father were already at the door. "We won't be needing your services anymore," she informed Miriam; then slammed the door behind them. My heart was pounding with anger.

"She can't get over that foot of hers," I managed. And I told Miriam about her cast and how she'd never been able to admit how it had humiliated her and set her apart.

Miriam made the generous offer of seeing me again, free of charge. I told her I appreciated the offer, but didn't feel right about it, and when I left her office a half hour later I was surprised by the feeling of friendship that gripped my throat and made it hard to say good-bye.

I expected tension when I arrived home, but was surprised to find my parents dressing to go out for dinner. They urged me to dress quickly and join them. I thought, maybe Miriam had made an impression, maybe my mother was sorry for what she'd said, or just felt better for saying it. But I thought, in the spirit of coexistence, it was best to accept and make concessions, or at least not disturb the respite.

I was startled by my parents' suggestion that we order drinks before dinner, and more startled still when we continued drinking throughout the meal. An unfamiliar and desperate intimacy found its way into our nostalgia. My mother brought up the time when my father had come back from the Korean War, his body mottled with boils, and how she would have to force him to get undressed in front of her, and how she'd use a washcloth on his back but she couldn't be gentle enough. He would try to hide the fact that he was crying, but his whole body was shaking with his sobs. And he said to her that he was crying not because of the pain, but because no one had ever shown him so much care.

And my mother asked if I remembered the time I was in elementary school and I wanted a pair of platform shoes like the teacher, Mr. Gutierrez, wore, and how she'd taken me out to get a pair even though she worried it would be bad for my feet. And I reminded her how my teacher, Mrs. O'Connor, southern trash that she was, had asked me to model them for the whole class while she told them only fairies wore shoes like that. My mother had stood up to Mrs. O'Connor then, and I was transferred to another class by the end of the day.

We told these stories as if to practice their success, to rehearse the feelings of resolve they each provided. One of us would take up the threads the other had thrown out, and so it was like an intangible weaving that transpired between us, like the sewing up of a fabric that had been unraveling. And by the time we had eaten our desserts and my father had assured us he could drive the few blocks back home, I had forgotten along with them the ugliness of the afternoon, and the months that had led up to it, and I told my mother that she looked more beautiful than I ever remembered her looking.

Late that evening, I sat listening to records in my room, feeling vaguely disquieted by our excursion to the restaurant, already thinking about how I would tell Miriam if I were to see her again. In some way, our levity and nostalgia felt like a betrayal of Miriam, as though the cloth we were weaving was to be put over our heads, blinding and deafening ourselves to what she had tried to say to my parents earlier that day.

I heard a quiet knocking at my door and my mother came into the room wearing her nightgown and slippers. She sat down next to me on the bed and took my hand in hers.

"You know," she said, "I just don't understand what it is you don't like about women." I pulled my hand from hers and sighed exasperatedly.

"Is it breasts?" she persisted, and this time I noticed her touching her own through the thin nightgown. "Are you worried that you couldn't please a woman? I've seen you in the shower—now don't be shy with me—you have a nice body. There are a lot of women out there who would be happy to have a man like you."

I felt trapped suddenly, and she took my hand again.

"What could I have done to make you fear women so much?" And with her other hand she dropped the strap of her nightgown and began to pull my hand toward her. I stared at her breast first with disbelief, then revulsion.

I twisted my hand from hers, saying very slowly and clearly, "Please get out of here."

When I'd pulled my hand from hers, she seemed almost to awaken and her expression was awkward and confused. She pulled the strap up on her nightgown and padded silently from the room, and I, shaking, locked the door behind her.

Months later, I was back to my same old tricks. My parents had discontinued their curfews and inquiries. My father had opened his own business and both he and my mother were concentrating on that. I was left to pursue my own pleasures.

One night, there was a large drag party planned at one of the clubs and I'd decided to dress for the event. That afternoon, while my parents were at work at the store, I went through my mother's closet. I thought it would be amusing and a little perverse to go as my mother. I found what had to be one of the ugliest dresses in her wardrobe, some synthetic green and white checkered dress with gold decorative buttons up the front. I was carefully going through her drawers for underwear and stockings when I discovered a plastic bag with something inside it. I sat on the floor before her dresser and opened the bag up on my lap. There, as new as the day they were delivered, were the plain, white baby shoes Mrs. Rosenbloom had brought to my bris. I felt suddenly stricken, shocked that she had kept them all these years. I put the shoes back in their bag and into the dresser, and then, sadly, I hung the dress back on the rack.

Undertow

The smell of cut grass and a tint of blue from the moon across its razed surface made me think of blood. I walked, well-dressed, across a wet, open field into an unfamiliar neighborhood where I'd been invited to a party. At the edge of the field, my elementary school stood squat, in darkness, finally small, arbitrary. Monkey bars in the distance looked like wire cages, domelike, sunk into the earth and the limestone beneath. I remembered watching my bicycle being stolen across this field. A teenager with an institutional walk, an apelike, slumping gait, carried it past, while I ran last and out of breath around the track. I stopped to watch him guide it away, intimidated by his sideburns and hairy arms. I was tearfully parting with the glowing red bike, its streamers from the handlebars lifeless and severed.

I was too afraid to say anything, until he'd gone—then the rush of real time, of consequence and loss, the sting of irremediable experience that would demand honest retelling, humbling repetition. Passing the school, small as a shoebox on the playing field, with portables like roach traps, bolted closets stacked with autoharps and recorders, I think of trapped voices, a clench of words, screams.

I slipped through a fence and crossed the street, into another field littered with cans and tires and magazine pictures. Three houses with gravel driveways sat in a cul-de-sac, yellow, blue, and pink, with ornate plaster seahorses chalk white against their walls. Cuban music played from a car outside the pink house. A man slumped in its front seat, smoking, feet on the dashboard. A heavyset girl stood outside the front door in a shirt of gathered popcorn fabric, kinky hair pulled back. It was her party, though most of her friends hadn't arrived. She had the worst English of anyone in our school. She was, they said, slow. I tutored her, and was the only non–Spanish speaker at her party.

She waved as I came up the gravel front, then stood before me, embarrassed by so few guests drifting apart in her heavily decorated living room: the whole ceiling like the skin of a piñata, a rough, short fringe; a crystal bowl with punch, orange sherbet marbling its surface. Rented lights and a DJ overwhelmed the room, especially with so few of us there; it made our hearts pound.

I went to the patio, and sat on a beach chair, now and then lifting the cover from the parrot's cage, fascinated by its angry wing beat, its ferocious quickness. I sat in the chair, nodding to people as they came out onto the patio, picking up pieces of their conversations, imagining Sonia and I as clairvoyant mutes, able to foretell the deaths of each of her guests. They would laugh at the message the way they laugh at the messenger. *Then, too bad for them.*

Leaning back in the patio chair, I thought of Key West. I was floating out over the hot backyard, flashes of green light and blue over the shrubs and trees, a tinted ocean of oil, the shrubs like stones jutting from it. I thought of my cousins, our playing in slow, elongated time, the long breathless dives and stretch of our bodies; my older cousin, whose body I watched for the past three years develop with rapidity against the slowness of our summers, like a swimmer against an undertow. I imagined the wet dark hair lying flat on his chest, tasting the salt of the water dried white on his body.

Then a group of boys arrived: older, beautiful, and imposing. Their presence in the living room sends people out on the patio. It is suddenly crowded, and I have to stand to see what's happening. People press against the patio screen, and some of the girls cover their eyes. I hear screaming and look out into the yard, flooded with light. A large pig ran through the yard, squealing, knocking into shrubs, while a gang of boys and men chased it with machetes. Some of the boys beside me laughed, holding their girlfriends like they do at movies, where squeamishness is sexual entreaty.

Someone brought the blade down on the hind leg of the animal and the crowd reacted with horror and laughter. The pig dragged itself across the yard, the perimeters shrinking. The blood in the floodlights was as dramatic and high as a fountain. My knees buckled. I slipped in sickness to the ground.

Sonia put me in her bed, under a pink and white comforter, strangely cakelike and girlish. She is neither soft nor feminine, but strong and ruddy. Being in her room is like playing doctor with her, dispensation to look inside, touch things you're not supposed to.

The door opens and a crowd of Cuban boys, just three or four years older than I, stand around the bed. They reach for me as though retrieving a coat. "Someone has to dance with Sonia," one says through a black mustache and gritted teeth.

They are like heads of the same monster, each face mesmerizingly beautiful. My eyes linger too long.

Another says, "Let's teach the faggot to dance." He is wearing a knit jersey; I see his gold medallions of saints under the cuts in his shirt. They pull me out to the living room where people are gathered, expectant. There are plantains frying in the kitchen. One of the boys pulls a pint of vodka from his back pocket and pours it into the punch; then ladles out a glass and tells me to drink.

They called Sonia out and pushed me beside her. She was thrilled, not understanding the spectacle we made—retarded girl and faggot. I'm thrown in the ring with something weaker. But her ignorance makes her powerful, natural. I stood woodenly against the music, colored by self-consciousness, a consciousness that comprehends everyone, the terrible probabilities of this amplified drunkenness. She began the Latin hustle to hoots and cheers. She took my hand and led. I could not match her rolling movements, the sensual slackening of her mouth, the low look of her eyes. Any expression of my being in my body would provoke the onlookers. She heard one of the boys comment, "*maricon*," and frowned in his direction. They laugh at her dawning awareness. One girl said, "Let's not watch anymore." When the music ended, I walked through the group of boys who were throwing wadded up, wet napkins. I called my father to pick me up. "So early?" he asked.

I stood in the gravel driveway, in night air that felt hot with my shame. I felt tapping all around me, lightly at first, then harder, more insistent. A rain of pebbles crashed over me, then a large stone hit the back of my head. "Good-bye faggot cocksucker," one boy said from the porch, flanked by two or three others. I felt the back of my head, the hair already wet, thick with blood. Another handful of stones. I found the large rock and picked it up, angry, facing them, but unable to throw it. "You throw like a girl," my father once said. He pulled his car up and stepped out of it, shocked by the blood on my hands. The boys don't stop at the sight of my father, but continue throwing stones at him, his car. He quickly guides me to the car and steps in. "What did you do?" he asks. The boys come off the porch and prance around the car, they are like phantoms, or rather, like cartoon natives around a cauldron. They are unreal. What is real is the blood from my father's eye sinking down his face into the velour seat of his Lincoln, and my pleading, "Nothing."

We'd board up the house with hurricane supplies before our drive to the Keys. We used corrugated aluminum sidings over the picture window, closed the awnings down over the bedroom windows, placed reinforcing pins in the sliding glass doors. We did this not for fear of hurricanes, but of marauding gangs, thieves, opportunists. That year my parents wouldn't go, my mother presiding over my father's eye, the stitching of his cornea, his head in her lap like an embroidery pattern. "Filthy," she spat. "Evil. No respect for anyone." My father reached a weak, consoling hand up to her face. She shooed it away, "Mac and Evie will take you," my mother said, referring to my aunt and uncle. "Your father and I have enough to worry about here."

For the first time, I am not to blame, not the provocateur. Guilt does not keep me from feeling satisfied that my father is hurt.

That night I dreamed I was crouched with my parents in a house of tin with a gravel floor. I'd found a buckle in the gummed seam of the tin wall and could see out. Naked boys circled the hut and were shooting through the tin with beebees which penetrated the walls with a reverberating ping; then a rush of coned light would invade the dwelling, illuminating our family, one at a time, in a shamed huddle.

Though we'd always left early in the morning for a road trip, I felt smuggled out that morning. My mother packed my bags the night before and placed them by the front door. She woke me at 4:30 A.M. and kissed me good-bye. I stood outside and there were still stars overhead, a strange, empty light that seemed to restore richness to the lawns and telephone posts, the well-spaced palms and flowering plants.

My uncle's car approached; the bleary headlights of his Valiant made the driveway look black and soft. My Aunt Evie rolled down the window and told me to get my bags and put them in the trunk. The distinct shrillness of her voice depressed me.

I looked through the back window expecting to see the odd shape of my cousin's head, now so familiar to me. Tom had a birth defect, a bubble at the back of his head that gave the impression his brain was split and half of it sat on the top of his skull. Unlike scalp, it was virtually hairless and webbed with veins, like the jellyfish we'd find at the beach and his brother Randy would stab with a stick. They'd had some success in reducing its size through early surgeries. And when he matured it became less pronounced. We were both thirteen. My heart sank at his absence. Except for Tom, they were all like strangers to me.

I opened the back door where my cousin Randy was pretending to be asleep, spread out over most of the back seat. I noticed for the first time the facial hair that seemed to make him so much older than the eighteen years he was. Both he and Tom had been adopted, but it was Randy's genes that seemed to possess a virulent teleology. He practically dwarfed my aunt and uncle, and had dark ruminative eyes and an almost disdainful expression to his mouth. The rest of the family were fair and light-eyed, even Tom. Each year Randy seemed less bound by the family, and my aunt and uncle conceded, perhaps out of fear, by granting him immunity to the rules they enforced on his brother.

"What's this?" Randy asked, pulling me by my necklace. It's a black lava tiki my parents brought back from Hawaii, with little fake red gems for eyes. It's a little bit of anger from a volcano. "It's good luck," I answered.

"That's really made from lava?" he asked. "That's pretty cool." He was already distracted by conch shell dealers set up on the roadside. "I wouldn't mind living like that," he said to the irritation of my aunt and uncle.

"Promise me we won't stop at Sugarloaf," he said, leaning forward, but really looking at himself in the rearview mirror. I saw the profile of my Uncle Mack flinching, his gaunt features patchy, like a fungus, and his nose bright red.

"This trip isn't just for you," he said. He stopped himself.

Randy folded his arms across his chest. "Too bad," he muttered.

"Where's Tom?" I asked.

"He's at a special school this summer," My aunt said.

"He's in the psych ward," Randy corrected, "studying beekeeping." He tittered, rubbing his open palms on his knees.

"Enough of you," my aunt said, turning in her seat and glaring at him. The eyebrows she'd drawn in looked like two exclamation points.

In Sugarloaf Key, we drove off the main road past a scuba rental shop. A dirt road stretched out to the water. All around us the land was barren except for tufts of brown grass. My uncle stopped the car in front of a cement-brick wall. The rest of us followed him out.

"By next year," he said, "we'll have a house here, and my boat will be tied over there." He pointed.

Randy looked restless already and was kicking the pyramids of red ants and bombing their cities with rocks. When he reached for one of the concrete bricks from the top of the wall, my aunt silently took his hand and squeezed it.

My uncle bought the property three years before, and every summer we'd come to visit the plot of land as though it were a gravesite. Now he wanted us to see it as a place we'd come to summer. "Key West," he would lament, "is becoming just a bunch of private beaches for fruits." There were no neighbors yet on this tiny Key. We stood there quietly for about fifteen minutes before my aunt said she wanted to use the bathroom, and so we went back to the main road. The visit depressed us all. When we finally pulled into a Chevron station, everyone's mood lifted.

Randy and I stayed in the car while my aunt and uncle went to the bathroom and brought cold drinks from the connected mart.

"Let me wear that," Randy demanded the moment they slammed their doors. He leaned over and began to remove the tiki from my neck. I let him. It lay flat against the hair on his chest. I reached out and turned it, making its eyes fire with sunlight. I want to spread his legs apart and crawl in closer to him, to let my hands explore under his shirt and up the legs of his shorts. "You can have it," I said, resting my eyes at the center of his chest.

"Too bad we can't fuck with Tom again," he said. I remembered guiding Tom under the pier, telling him Randy wanted us to see something he'd found. The water under the pier was cold and the stones slick with algae. Randy stood beside a leaning piece of seawall, as though it were a large trophy. I could hear the scuttling behind it, stepping back in anticipation of the surprise. When Tom had ventured close enough, Randy toppled the piece of wall and hundreds of blue crabs scrambled off the slippery surface. Tom was beating wildly in the water, a few of the crabs clamped onto him like swinging ornaments. I remember being stunned by how upset he'd become. Later I'd apologized for laughing at him, but it had never ceased being funny to

Randy and me. We'd whispered about it from bed to bed after Tom had fallen asleep. I asked Randy about the parties he went to, the girls he met and how far he'd gone with them. Their behavior fascinated and troubled him. I wanted to ask him how it felt when he kissed them, where he touched them, how they responded. I wanted to offer myself for practicing on—silent and compliant as a pillow.

Instead, I asked him about night swimming, about the powerful undertow that made it off-limits to Tom and me—could he feel it dragging him off course, swallowing his resistance?

We crossed the Seven Mile Bridge under blinding sunlight. It seemed frighteningly insubstantial, stretching out over the ocean's rough, glinting surface and contradictory currents.

"Some good fishing ahead," my uncle said. Now he had sunglasses and a thick, white cream on his nose. I knew he was suggesting this to Randy; on the last trip he'd caught me throwing their catch off the boat.

I couldn't explain my dread of fishing. The gills were the most horrible part, like perfect incisions, pulsing like just-cleaned cuts, sucking hard as though attempting to draw the moisture from the air. Randy would run his fingers through the gills, or slide the fish across the floor of the boat where they'd collect, tails still beating, once a graceful motility. Their mouths would bubble out with gray fish gut, their eyes fixed like glass.

Benevolence in their family was ascribed to Tom—the otherworldliness in him— something serene and reserved he'd developed, perhaps, from the odd shape of his head. He'd once taken a sick bird from a classroom incubator and fed it from a dropper around the clock; then named it Garlic after it had pecked at some, and dizzyingly, comically, staggered from the plate. The bird always remained frightened and small and incapable of flight. It became a creature of the palm rather than one of the air.

In two months it was dead, strangled in Randy's shoelace in his attempt to make a leash for it. He'd killed Garlic by mistake. He'd never meant to; it was a kind of brutal curiosity he developed around helpless things.

Tom shrank away from him—a reflex. He moved from puzzles to computers, normal interests. But I couldn't take my eyes off Randy, flattering him with discreet observation, watching his hand play over himself from the other bed, an observation that seemed to encourage him, creating almost a schedule, like a film that starts up when the viewer arrives. Except, of course, when he was at the ocean, night swimming, or guiding girls beneath the piers or around the poolside while their parents slept.

Once I watched him through a slit in the curtains kissing a girl we'd seen at the beach. I watched their figures circling in the cold pool light, all the windows dark, with my hand like a visor to the glass, until I was certain he was watching me, and the two stood only feet away, his kissing merely a distraction from the work of his hands. I watched him clutch her top and tear it down, and stand behind her with his hand over her mouth. He held her hand behind her back and turned her toward the window, her breasts heaving, her back painfully arched, reacting to his kisses like bites, a look about her like Tom's with the crabs clamped to him, an almost comic fear, an awkward resistance. I watched her break away from him, and run out to the street.

We arrived at the hotel where we always stayed, the Santa Maria. The owner, Abdallah, brought his face down to the window, smiling broadly at my aunt and uncle. He took my aunt's hand into his own and kissed it, a strange formality or humorous extravagance he'd carried from Morocco. I rolled my window down and threw my arms around his neck. I loved the scratchiness of his short beard and the limey smell of his cologne.

"Where's Ahmed?" I asked. His son and I played together. Although I often found him boring, it was an excuse to be near his father in their apartment. They lived in the hotel in a room behind the lobby mailboxes. The small apartment always smelled of spices and coffee, and of chlorine from their wet bathing suits hanging in the sunlit window. Ahmed's mother had died of cancer, so it was just the two of them, which seemed exotic to me. His father was dark and muscular and rarely wore a shirt. He watched their small television with just his shorts and sandals on. Ahmed would spread his coin collection over the rug, but I never concentrated on it. My eyes would go from the profiles on the coins to his father's. His nose was long, his eyelashes thick and ink black. His lips were the bright pink of the inside of a conch shell, and always looked soft and glossed and taken care of.

"Ahmed is away at Seacamp for the summer," he said. Then rubbing my head with the palm of his hand, "Come and look at his coins whenever you want."

I felt a glow of shame come over me. His invitation felt like a seduction. I imagined the lingering of his callused palm over my face, the soft punctuation of his lips on mine. Suddenly Ahmed's disengaged presence meant everything—the bottle thickness of his glasses and his immersion in coins, his books on sea life. Normal interests. I was faced with my own naked infatuation. I remembered the year before, walking around the poolside in my bathing suit, thinking Ahmed's father could see me from the reservations desk. Brutally, my father had called my attention to the way I wiggled like a girl, which I blamed on my thongs.

Randy and I had our own room. His parents, in an adjoining room, slept in separate beds, the way they did at home.

My mother had told me not to mention it. I watched them unpack at opposite sides of the room. I'd marveled at how they'd divided their responsibilities by each claiming one child. Randy was Mack's child; Tom was Evie's. With Tom away that summer, I could feel the divide of their affections—my aunt's quiet, elderly doting, and my uncle's almost complete disengagement from me. Randy's privilege had always stemmed from this arrangement—favoritism from the head of the household. Tom's indulgence was mother love, a sympathetic accommodation that rendered him impossibly shy around men.

Randy informed his father he'd take the car that night, and Uncle Mack, still folding swim trunks and putting them neatly in a drawer by his bed, consented wordlessly. I followed Randy from their room into ours. He closed the adjoining door and locked it. "I want to go tonight," I told him pleadingly.

"Maybe some other time. Besides, my mom won't let you go."

"She's not *my* mom," I said despondently. "I could sneak out."

"Not tonight," he said, turning from the mirror to look at me. "I'll tell you all about it when I get back."

That night I walked through the glass-walled lobby of the Santa Maria, the sky mixing orange and dark blue as the sun dropped out of sight behind the ocean. There were only a couple of people inside the bar, the jukebox played "There's A Kind of Hush." The lobby, with its oversized coral-colored chairs, was empty. I sat in different chairs, first looking out toward the empty pool; then facing the street where some bicyclists were making their way down toward the beach. I imagined Randy and his friends in dark water, clothes piled at the shore, their bodies drifting together like buoys, the movement of their hands hidden beneath the tumbling breath of waves.

I walked to Abdallah's door and knocked, suddenly anxious. He answered it in shorts. I looked directly at the deep brown creases around his stomach.

"Come in," he welcomed. He went to his son's coin collection and withdrew it from a closet shelf. He placed the trays down on the carpet next to his recliner, and put his feet back up, facing the television. His hand drifted down from the armrest and patted my head; then began a thoughtless kind of stroking as he might have done to a cat on his lap. I slowly let my head respond to his hand, rolling it against his palm. The coins remained untouched before me, currencies removed from exchange, just the warm glow of their surfaces and the weight of them.

Randy came in drunk that night; he fell into his bed with sand on his feet and in the hair on his legs. He didn't turn the light on, just removed his shorts and shirt and dropped them by the side of the bed. He lay on the bed with his arms over his head, watching the play of light from the pool on the ceiling. "You awake?" he asked after a while.

"Yes," I answered. "What happened?"

"Come here and I'll tell you." He looked away.

I crawled into his bed. Up close to him, the hair under his arms looked thick with sweat. "What'd you do?" I asked. His profile was like stone, mottled by short, coarse hair, his lips barely parted, as though his teeth were clenched.

"I fucked some girl," he said. I see his hand travel under the sheet, a moving knot, toward his groin. I remembered playing with cats and dogs that way, hypnotizing them with the thing under the sheet, at the same time protecting myself from their bites and scratches.

"How'd you do it?" I asked, putting my head beneath the sheet, not needing an answer, smarter than a dog.

I felt his hand clamp to the back of my neck and force me toward his crotch. I reached out for his penis, already hard and gripped by his other hand, but he more insistently moved my mouth to it. The unpracticed act felt nonetheless inevitable, and I approached with anxiousness and dread; I opened my mouth and felt his hips jerk up to deliver it, his hand (and mine) fell away. My eyes and nose were greedy, too, as though instinctively committing it to memory. I breathed in, and the smell of saltwater and the sweat of his crotch commingled. The sight of that part of his cock that wasn't in my mouth; his testicles, still hanging fully between his parted legs; and the thrust of his hips became permanent, a moment upon which all others would build. But almost fighting this memorial, his hips swing into violent thrusts, rolling over and straddling my head as though it's a pillow, oblivious to my gagging, the tears forced from my eyes. He whispers, "sshhh," an exhalation of the breath he's stolen from me, and then, lifting out of my throat, but still in my mouth, shoots his semen in cathartic bursts, drowning me in the salt of his violence and his pleasure. Before I've even swallowed it, he's pushed me off the bed and onto the floor. For a moment I remain there watching him; he's unconcerned even with my humiliation, and falls to sleep with no softening of his features.

I went to my bed and watched him, angered, perhaps by how little he reveals, the invulnerability of his desire and the wretched expression of mine. He sleeps safe and unconcerned; I watch, protecting him from nothing. And it is the feeling of nothing that has become an enemy of mine.

For days Randy wouldn't speak to me. He was never in his family's company, but stayed out from early in the morning until late night. When he'd walk into the room, my breathing would go shallow. I'd put the blankets in my mouth to silence the thin panic, the pang of lust like fists to the stomach. He undressed always facing my bed, and my eyes, with a developed sensitivity to the darkness, could make out the muscles of his stomach and the slight movements of his half-hard penis, fixing this image of him there so that it remained standing at the edge of his bed while he covered himself and slept. I would imagine him naked, walking toward me, secretively, until this image dissolved, just before touching me.

Then, the night before we were to leave Key West, he put his head in the door and told me to come outside. I jumped from my place in front of the television and followed him out. It was probably eight in the evening, but the poolside was empty and the pool lights were on, illuminating the mosaic at its depths. Randy patted a seat and held his finger to his mouth. We were sitting at a large, umbrella-topped table, Randy's legs outstretched before him.

"You're just in time," he whispered, nodding in the direction of a window across the way. "Check out the floor show." In the window, a woman in her late thirties was standing with her top off and wearing only the barest g-string bikini bottom. Her breasts looked triangulated from the abrupt tan line, her nipples standing out hard from the white skin.

"How long have you been watching her?" I asked.

He was intent on her image; my words were flies around his head. He batted them away.

"I'd like to fuck her good," he said in a voice almost menacing. I remembered him holding Tom's face down in a sawdust pit, forcing him to eat from it. Now the woman was sliding off the g-string.

"She's showing us her pussy," he said, and the towel over his crotch started to jump. I was afraid to look at the window, but Randy was bold. He sat back, shamelessly rubbing the towel. "Look at that," he said, perusing violently the thing in the window, commenting on her parts like the opened back of a beef truck.

"Check her out, she's looking at you." He challenges me to take my eyes off him. In a cursory glance I see her naked in a chair, one leg thrown over the side, the fingers of one hand lost between her legs. She's smoking with the other hand. In that instant, my embarrassment seemed to threaten her; she turned her head and blew smoke, as if casually, into the indistinct darkness behind her. It was like watching myself sashay along the poolside in a home movie projected by my father. I wondered if I always appeared as overt as the woman in the window, as hard to look at.

Randy could look at it.

I was flooded with memories that seemed suddenly to expose me—a kiss I'd given another cousin at his wedding that lingered far too long, a game of strip checkers I'd played with two other boys after sending Tom out of the room. When I met up with him later, he seemed not even mildly curious about who had won or lost, or how, in my case, the losing had meant winning.

The woman stepped behind the curtain flashing a last brief smile at Randy. Randy was ecstatic when she turned her light off and drew the curtains. He wanted to get drunk, he told me, and go to her room later. In my desperateness to be useful to him, my mind races like a dog retrieving slippers for its master. "I can get you the key to her room."

Randy looks skeptically at me. "How?" he asks.

"If I get it," I say, "you have to promise to take me to the ocean tonight."

"I'll even get you drunk."

"And let me go night swimming," I insist.

"I'll let you get as crazy as you want, little pecker, just get me that key."

I tell him to wait in the lobby, and watch him go into the Castaways bar and take a seat on one of the barstools. I walk over to Abdallah's door and knock. I knock again, this time with a sinking feeling that he is not home, or is asleep, or that he has seen me from the peephole in the door and has decided not to answer. Then I hear the sound of the lock and see him there in the doorway wearing only his boxer shorts and a gold chain around his neck.

"Isn't it late for you?" he asks. "Come in."

"I just wanted to look at some coins for a few minutes," I tell him.

He opens the closet door where the keys to each room are mounted. He brushes against them when he stretches up to bring down a tray of coins. We walk toward the television and I take my place on the rug beside his chair. He sighs as he settles back into it. His sexiness is lost to his generosity, to the benign mystery of the coins he offers me.

"Where does this one come from?" I ask, feigning interest the way I used to with his son. I'm grateful when he doesn't answer; it suggests he may not want to move to put them back. I put one like a monocle to my eye and turn to face him. I contrive it, something his son had once done. For a moment he looks down at me, shakes his head at the antic, and returns his attention to the set. I imagine Randy's impatience, and feel it for Abdallah, whose kindness seems oafish suddenly. Like Sonia, he doesn't speak the language, doesn't recognize his part in predation.

"I'll put this back," I say.

"You can't reach it can you?" he asks, not turning as I carry it to the closet.

"Of course I can," I say, my eyes scanning the keys, the room numbers written over the many hooks on the whitewashed board. I take her key the instant I find it, and, still holding the tray, reach up to put it on the shelf. Keys are more powerful than coins; I think at that moment, perhaps I'll collect them. He turns just as I pocket it in my shorts. He looks suspiciously at me. "I hope if you're borrowing a coin you'll bring it back tomorrow."

"No," I answer, "I'm not borrowing anything." I turn my pockets out and dangle the key before him. "Just my room key."

He turns back toward the TV. "Don't stay out too late."

"I can't believe you," Randy said, as I put the key into his hand. He put his arm around my neck, the key in his fist. "I'll creep in there and give her what she's asking for," he tightened his rein on my neck, his lips almost brushing my ear. "Let's go get that alcohol I promised."

I am not jealous of the woman, or worried for her.

We walked from the hotel, and while still quite a distance from the beach, could hear the sound of waves along the seawall.

We walked toward a market, almost like a shack with a portable generated sign boasting "Liquors." Beside Randy I felt part of a gang, as though he had the crowding power of that roomful of Cuban boys. The stretch of road was empty, and I thought, here comes the hurricane, everyone stay inside. He left me while he went inside the store. I listened to the ocean crash against the wall.

We headed down toward the sound, Randy drinking beside me. He handed the flask-shaped bottle to me, challenged me. He tossed the empty bottle in the sand and opened another. "Whisky'll keep you warm out here," he said, walking backward along the surf. He climbed up on a rock, put his hands behind his head and stretched himself out over it, looking up at a black sky pricked with stars. Suddenly he began to howl and I noticed then the moon, remote, allowing the tides to go out of control. I started to feel uneasy as his howling grew louder, but when I made a turn to move away from him, he gripped my arm.

"What about your swim?" he asked. His laugh was as loud as the roar of waves. I was so drunk I felt my knees buckle. I remembered Tom with those crabs clinging to him. I couldn't get that foolish dance out of my head.

"What about it?" he asked, amused by something he wasn't sharing. "Go ahead, I'll watch you."

"I didn't bring a bathing suit," I answered, my voice lost to the wind and the crash of waves.

"Take your clothes off," he said, "you know you want to."

I took my shirt and shoes off and put them on the rock beside him. I took off my shorts and underwear next. My body, covered with goose bumps, disappointed me. It was just a kid's body, shriveled with cold, and clumsy with so little alcohol.

"Go on," he said. "See if you can swim out to that ship." He pointed to what looked like a tanker not far from the horizon, a ghost ship.

Under his scrutiny, I walked to the waves and stopped quickly at the first feel of icy water on my toes. I felt the sand breaking up beneath my feet, dissolving. I awkwardly took my first steps into the water, my hands out before me as though I was walking into a place without light. I drew in a deep breath and bent into the water. Under the surface, my arms and legs were fighting in slow motion. I was withdrawing from the shore, just my head moving out over the huge cresting waves. I was exhilarated but exhausted, too, and just let myself rise and fall with the waves. I stretched out my toes as though I expected to feel the undertow my parents had always warned me of, pulling at each of my toes, one at a time, before sucking me under suddenly.

I stayed out for some time, until my bobbing became effortless. But the water got cold again without my effort against it, as though it was charged with memories of another me altogether, wordless, out on the playing field behind my school. I called out to Randy, to lure him in. "There is no undertow." That's how drunk I was, because I kept shouting it even as I watched him walking up the beach and disappearing out onto the main road.

The Medicine Burns

I see my pitted skin reflected in the tinted window of the airport limousine. Outside, the flat, white fields appear endless; my reflection is an overlay of holes. The landscape has other blemishes, dead trees here and there, an old farmhouse half sunk in the snow. Beneath the snow, I can just make out the dead, wiry stalks of corn combed back across the land, parted, it seems, like frozen hair.

We enter town as the lights of Old Capital are turned on. I see its gold dome from a distance. The driver points out the English and Philosophy building from his window. It is an old brownstone and unlike anything I've known in Miami. We drive up to the front of Stonecourt Apartments; I am overwhelmed with disappointment. The building is far from the campus, off the side of the highway. It looks like a dorm; less attractive than the dorms he'd pointed out on the way over here. I want to ask him to keep driving.

There's an information area near the banks of elevators. The attendant greets me eagerly, as though he's hemmed in by the counter.

"You're very lucky," he tells me as he slides the rental agreement over the counter. "The tenant before you mirrored one of his walls so you have the only different apartment in the building."

As I sign my name to several sheets of paper, he leans over and whispers, "The guy who lived there was kind of kinky, I think."

I look at him, disinterested, and return the papers to him. There is nothing outstanding about his face; it is as common as the faces coming off the elevators. I find it both pathetic and enviable. Some people look like they belong, even in places like this.

"I live here, too," he says, and I notice his braces for the first time. They don't surprise me on children, but on him they're shocking.

"Maybe I'll check up on you later," he warns, "just to make sure you've got everything you need."

The mirrors are cheap tiles affixed to the wall next to the bed. My first instinct is to pull the bed away from the wall. I can't imagine rolling over in the morning and seeing myself right away.

I turn away from the mirrors as I make my way around the foot of the bed, but I detect an image from the corner of my eye, a presence I can never completely obliterate, hunched over, almost hiding, and wearing a blue shirt.

I meet Lawrence on the first day of class. He's smoking in the hallway, dressed beautifully, sure of himself. I ask him if this is where Theory and History of the Avant Garde will be taught. He nods. I look out the window at the slick walkways and I can feel his eyes on me.

"Is this your first semester?" he asks, more curious than the question permits. My face can do that sometimes, encourage curiosity. He has the striking beauty of a face you see in a magazine, looks, I am sure, that enable him to have whatever he wants.

We sit together in class, in the last row so we can talk while the professor shows slides. He asks me where I'm staying and when I mention the Stonecourt Apartments he whispers, "I'm sorry. There's a suicide there every winter." Then, "If I had to live there, I'd jump too, but from the penthouse."

When the lights are off, he seems relieved and leans back in his seat. He leans in toward me and whispers, "Brancusi's *The New Born*." The projected sculpture is perfectly smooth. The professor extracts a long, silver pointer from what looks like a pen. He cannot resist its surface and absently traces it while he lectures.

"He's passionate about his subject," Lawrence says, sounding ironic, jealous even of that work of art.

"You must have had him before?" I ask.

"Oh, yes," he says, "too often."

I look closely at the professor. He is thin but distinguished with a shock of gray hair at the front of his part, which someone, my mother probably, told me had to do with kidney dysfunction. Between him and Lawrence, I begin to suspect a conspiracy of elegant, wealthy men sprinkled throughout the general population of students, but the function of this secret fraternity is difficult to discern.

On the break, Lawrence tells me his full name, Lawrence Coolidge III. He must be joking, but I don't question it; there is something about him that makes me think, cynically, of the word *breeding*. He tells me that he is a painter and that his family lives in

Chicago; he has been a student here in Iowa for two years. I've never been to Chicago; all my images of it are derived from *Sister Carrie*.

"I'm in the English Department," I mention. I decide not to tell him about my own failed attempts at painting. Even simple figure or perspective drawing is profoundly difficult for me. I don't trust my eye enough; I am always embellishing.

Maybe the secret club of beautiful men casts light on the ugly ones. I can imagine Lawrence and the professor shrunk down and in a glowing halo at the corner of my room watching me slide out of bed after I'd attempted sex with the information-booth attendant.

He looks so haggard under the standing lamp near my bed. He sits on the edge of my bed in discolored underwear and nylon socks, his brittle yellow body slumped with a shame I cannot rid him of.

I suppose that is what I am trying to do. I continue to disgrace myself in making him feel wanted. I'll often beg him to deliver his tongue to me through his wired mouth. He obliges me with a power he is unaware of. He is even more powerful when he doesn't oblige.

He is a codeine addict, and I've spent the afternoon driving around with him filling forged cough medicine prescriptions. There are three sticky bottles in the garbage can, one half-full on the night table. When I look at the red ring on the table, I can practically feel it on my skin. It feels like his presence, but though I'd like to be rid of him, I have my own addictions.

He flicks off the light, and until my eyes adjust, there is only the sound of him scratching his skin. He does this obsessively. My only relief is not seeing it.

"I wish you'd let me play my Hank Williams, Jr. record for you," he says sleepily. "I think you'd like it."

"How many times have I told you I hate country music and country people?" I am rigid in the dark.

I see his hand sliding from the side of the bed, searching out his guitar lying on the floor. The first two nights he spent with me, I had mistakenly told him I liked his playing. He told me he liked to sing me to sleep, and so I'd pretended with my eyes closed. But he could go on singing for an hour at least.

I grab his hand and twist it until I hear him whimpering. "No playing tonight," I say through clenched teeth.

He finally falls asleep while I sit propped against the opposite wall. I'm so tense I can't sleep. I concentrate on matching my breathing to his so that I can forget he's there.

I vow that I won't sleep with him again, and stretch out on the floor without cover or pillow. But my vow does not dispel my closet of skeletons, ugly burdensome men I've broken every taboo to meet. They hang there, as patient without me as they were with me. I am a bad medicine, I think. I do not heal them, and they discard me even when they are terminal cases and there's nothing else.

They hang there: the old ones, the amputees, the mentally retarded. I'd like to cut their ropes so they could fall with all the suicides of this building. I imagine them in a sordid heap at the lobby doors of the Stonecourt Apartments, their bodies like a barricade against the doors.

Lawrence invites me to his apartment which is a large one-bedroom in a wooded area behind the campus. It's a quaint setting with a wooden bridge which crosses a landscaped ravine. We stop for a moment on the bridge, and look down at the thin brook trickling over black stones.

"Almost like wilderness," he says, "but they can trip floodlights and light up the whole set." He points out some of the lights, discreetly positioned behind trees. "A woman was raped here a few years ago. Now the place is like a laid trap."

"I'll watch where I step," I assure him.

I distrust the moonlight that makes his features take on the strange, alien quality of the man-made brook. It makes the thought of touching him seem odd and cold.

He opens the door to his apartment and ushers me inside. There is an awkward feeling as we stand, hesitant, in the doorway, as though he were housesitting with instructions not to bring in guests. He takes my coat and the warmth of the room envelops me.

"Have a seat," he says, aware of my awkwardness. I sit down on an elegant, forest green couch. He tells me he'll get coffee and turns the radio on before he leaves the room. It's the classical music station playing softly Vaughan Williams's "Fantasia On A Theme."

"Do you know this piece?" I ask him.

"No," he calls out from the kitchen. "I don't really like classical music."

This is the apartment of someone established, I think, not a student. The room is rosy and wood-rich, too designed, too considered even for a student with wealthy parents. When he returns with coffee, I can't help but admire the way he moves around the place so comfortably, like an impostor.

"There's a man I've been seeing since I first moved here. He pays the rent on this place. I had him over last weekend. This is the radio station he likes to listen to. I don't listen to the radio when I'm here alone," he says nonchalantly. I notice, though, that he seems to be looking for a response, either shock or forgiveness.

For a moment, I don't know what I feel. Maybe envy.

"Do you love him?" I ask.

Lawrence looks at me as though I'm insane. Then his eyes soften a little. "I respect him," he says.

Lawrence insists on taking me by his studio. "It's on your way home." He gathers his coat.

He is one of the few students with his own studio in the painting building. The others stand in a large, open area at easels.

There is a padlock on the door and his initials, minus the III, painted on the wall. Inside, the space is crowded with canvases. Two of them are hanging on the wall, illuminated by a clamp light. I walk up close to them, surprised both by their accuracy and their beauty. They are self-portraits, simply and elegantly rendered. In one of the portraits he is looking into a mirror the way I never could, searching it as though it held the truth.

I turn to him. "They're beautiful," I tell him, and it's easier than admitting he is.

I stand at the center of my apartment in disbelief. Practically nothing has been opened or arranged. I begin cutting the tape on an earlier life comprehensively packed and already musty smelling and foreign.

I am uncomfortable putting out the books and records and posters. They seem frighteningly self-conscious now, as though I had gone out of my way to compensate, by way of taste, for a lack in appearance. The whole life is made up. I'm afraid that Lawrence will see through my obsession with the grotesque in film, my collections of criticism and philosophy. He will see just an ugly person filling in the holes.

I leave the boxes packed, the clothes neatly folded. I stand before the mirror tiles, stretching out my skin until it looks almost smooth. My hands move section by section over my face; I cover it all except for my eyes, peering out between my fingers.

I remember when I couldn't touch my face. It was two years after I had discontinued a violent dermatological therapy. My face was so red and disturbed I had grown afraid to touch it. The last doctor I saw, at the tearful request of my mother, was an old, Jewish hunchback who had an office in downtown Miami.

He took me into the bathroom and stood behind me and taught me how to wash my face. He held onto my hands and gently guided them over my cheeks and forehead. All along, I made him promise not to inject anything into my skin, not to use chemical peels. He stood behind me whispering, "Only pills, no pain."

In my room, the ghosts rise from the boxes like dust. I feel my parents' hands on my throat and feet. They, too, are pleading.

"Can't you do something about your face?" my mother asks disdainfully. "Wash it again," she insists, "you've got time."

"But I have washed it." I want her to notice that I'm wearing my new blazer and tie. But she only sees my face, stinging and burning from the medicine that puts holes in the pillowcase.

I close the boxes and start to pack them away in the closet. I sit down with the last box, though. It's packed with books. I draw one out and open it on my lap. It is a poem by Rupert Brooke, and I begin to recite it quietly to myself.

And I knew
That this was the hour of knowing,
And the night and the woods and you
Were one together, and I should find
Soon in the silence the hidden key
Of all that had hurt and puzzled me—
Why you were you, and the night was kind,
And the woods were part of the heart of me.

And there I waited breathlessly,
Alone; and slowly the holy three,
The three that I loved, together grew
One, in the hour of knowing,
Night, and the woods, and you—

Lawrence is at the door. I tell him to come in quickly, fearful the attendant might be loitering in the hall.

"I think I've been drinking," he says. I have him sit on one of the two rotating chairs that the apartment came furnished with. The chairs are covered in loud, flower-printed vinyl and look like hotel liquidation from the seventies. "Don't you have any chairs that sit still?" he asks.

I offer him coffee, and by the time I bring out a mug, he has found his way to the mirrored wall.

He opens up to me recklessly, "I'm sleeping with our professor, you know."

"Really? Is he good?" I ask.

"Lousy," he says. "He treats me like a work of art, touches me with a white glove, centers me on the bed and asks me not to move."

"He asks you not to move and doesn't have the decency to tie you up?"

"No way," he laughs. "He won't even use a collar on his dog."

"And he's not the one who pays your rent?" I ask.

"No," he says, becoming more serious. "That's Ray." He swoons a little, the alcohol showing. "I'm starting to worry about their paths crossing. Last weekend, while Ray was over, the professor kept calling, saying he knew I was there."

"Boy," I say, my voice sounding surprisingly mocking, "what a mess."

"I was counting on your understanding," he says conspiratorially.

"Shall I seduce him?" I ask.

Lawrence laughs. "He goes for the pretty boys," he says in a way that makes me think I shouldn't feel hurt.

It dawns on me suddenly that he sees me as clearly as he does himself. He is beautiful and I am ugly. How could I have ever imagined those lines between us blurring?

"What do you want me to do?" I ask, knowing his answer. He wants me to play the ugly role.

Just then I hear knocking at my door. "Oh God," I say under my breath.

"Please let me in," the attendant says through the chain.

"Get lost," I say bitterly.

"I know you have someone over. I just need to come in for a minute," he croaks.

"What for?" I ask, reddening.

"I need to get my cough medicine," he says.

"I'll get it."

I pick up the gluey bottle from the night table and uncap it. I stick my hand out of the crack of the door and pour the red liquid over his hands and on the rug. He stands there startled as though it were blood. When I look back at Lawrence, he is laughing.

I'm freezing out here, crouched in the shadow of the bridge. I see the professor's car driving slowly up the path and sink lower into the brush, pulling it over me like a blanket. I do this carefully, suddenly remembering the banks of lights trained on me. I imagine tripping the system and the ravine flooding with light, but there are only two beams quickly extinguished when he pulls into the driveway. My breathing seems to me too loud, and even though I try to calm myself, it is all I hear in the woods. And then I hear his door open, his feet on the gravel and up on the wooden porch. I crawl up closer to see him under the porch light. He stands there looking down at his feet after he rings the bell. He looks so gentle and patient and in love, I think, waiting to be let inside.

He steps into the doorway and it is as if a meter begins to tick away. I recognize it then as my heart. Lawrence pulls the shade down, and as we agreed, I begin to move towards the door, opening it quietly and letting myself in. I feel them instantly with the acute senses of an animal. Lawrence spots me from the bedroom (did he see me too soon?). I begin talking over the chaos.

"Oh my God," I say shocked. "I can't believe this."

Lawrence looks at me stunned (it is not very convincing, but the professor isn't looking at him. It is my moment.)

Lawrence asks, "Why didn't you knock?"

"I just didn't," I say, beginning to feel real agitation. "I didn't expect to catch you in a private tutorial."

The professor is in his pants already, sliding on his glasses. He looks at me with wide, frightened eyes. It is our hope that he'll recognize me from class, but I don't see any recognition in his eyes. Only fear, as though I am a monster, some Bigfoot that lives in the ravine.

"I have to go," he says nervously. He is still looking at me when he says it. He starts to leave without his tan jacket. I hand it to him at the door. I am feeling so powerful, I give him a little push from behind. He turns angrily toward me.

"You've got nothing on me," he says, voice trembling, looking into my eyes. Then he must have seen something there that made him turn and go.

I think my face has changed. Not healed, but settled. Reinforced. Lawrence calls my face scary. He says there is something intimidating about it, and he loves to recall the way I looked on the night with the professor. "It was almost like a jealous lover had walked in," he says.

"It's been a week since you've heard from him," I say, "so I guess it worked."

"It worked beautifully," he says. "I wasn't complaining." But he looks at me sharply, and it seems for a moment that instead of me, he's looking at a small flaw on the couch.

"Ray's wife is leaving town for the next month," he says, "and Ray's asked me to stay at his place to help him work on the nursery. Rosemary's pregnant and Ray's already acting like a proud father."

"What's he grooming you for? A nanny position?" I sound like that scary person Lawrence finds amusing. "Why is he moving you in?" I ask, grasping.

He talks to me with his back turned, going into the kitchen. "He has a big, beautiful house. While she's gone, we're going to use it." His words sound so simple; it is like he is explaining it to a child.

"I wonder what it's like to have someone take care of you."

Lawrence calls out casually from the kitchen, "I didn't think you were the romantic type."

Why, then, do I feel excluded from him? Why do I feel left out of the happy family—Lawrence, Ray, and his pregnant wife?

But he emerges from the kitchen with a bottle of sherry and two glasses. Either to calm the panic he hears rising in me, or in genuine appreciation, he toasts to our friendship. I look into his eyes. Strangely, the closer he gets to me, the more remote I find him. I wonder if that is how it works with Ray.

It's gotten so that I can't think of Lawrence without Ray somewhere in the background. It's like when someone you know has cancer, how it's always there. It's not like Lawrence talks about him, about what they do, or how they feel about each other. It's just his name with a time and place written next to it under a magnet on the refrigerator, or his voice coming from the phone machine in Lawrence's bedroom. Whenever the phone rings, I always ask "who's that?" as though I'm waiting for his call.

Lawrence explains that I can leave messages for him and he'll call me from Ray's house. "I'll just be a few blocks away," he says, comforting me. But I can't seem to rid myself of the chill of that ravine, knowing this time I'll be locked out without a plan.

It is by chance that I've spotted him and Ray tonight coming out of The Mill. I would walk up to them and shake Ray's hand if they weren't so engaged in talk. Lawrence just keeps looking over to him, as though he is never going to see him again, as though he is trying to memorize his face.

I follow at a great distance. They walk together without touching until they start over the railroad bridge; then Ray takes Lawrence's gloved hand and guides him across, and it seems as natural as a father and child.

I am terrified of heights, and the bridge is no easy feat for me. It is not a footpath, merely an old railroad track that runs over some reinforcing beams. There is nothing to hold onto, except the track itself. I cross it on all fours. Far below, the water is frozen, certain death if I slip.

It takes me so long to cross the bridge, I feel certain I've lost them. Then, cutting across College Green Park, I see them again entering a sky blue, wooden house on the corner. The snow is lightly falling, and the perfect little house looks like a Christmas card.

I wonder what it is like to be pursued by an admirer, to be watched, investigated, loved.

Did Lawrence have to pursue anyone? Lawrence doesn't need to do anything, I tell myself, but I need to do everything.

Suddenly, the front door opens. Ray comes off the porch and looks up momentarily. I'm leaning against the oak, in the snow, with my ski hat on. I stand there casually turning a stick in my hands. He locates my eyes and glances away.

He pulls up the door of the garage and opens the passenger door of his truck. I see him removing a large roll of paper from the seat, then he takes a plastic bucket out of the back of the truck and carries them back into the house.

The garage is wide open. I stand there for a while looking at it. I am already walking out of the park and crossing the street. I've done crazier things, I assure myself, and I conjure up the feeling of power I felt pushing the professor out into the cold.

I glance over all the windows of the house, no movements, no one looking out. I hurriedly walk up to the garage. I feel safe once I'm inside, and begin to look over his things: his work table and saw, his toolbox, and the coils of extension cords hanging from hooks in the wall. It's a regular shop in here, I think, wondering if there is anything small I can take. I turn my attention to his truck, and there, as though he were offering them to me, are his keys dangling from the lock in the passenger door.

The moment they're in my hands I feel spooked and have to leave.

Lawrence calls. He's been at Ray's for two weeks, but he's alone tonight. He talks about the snow and how it makes him feel like a child, the one that felt trapped in his parents' house, an old Chicago house full of rugs and clocks and his father's pipe smoke. While he talks, I look out my window at the highway stretching north and the snow passing over all of it, the kind of lonely sight that makes people jump every winter, and I say, "It sounds safe and warm in your old house."

"That's why I never left," he answers.

We've come to Pete's, a small bar with pool tables and wooden booths, where it's not hard to be anonymous. There are just Pete and the two of us.

He's wearing jeans and a down jacket that is obviously not his. I remember us laughing about down jackets and how they looked like potholders. I don't mention it.

"It's difficult spending so much time at Ray's," he says thoughtfully, pouring beer from the pitcher. "I'm afraid I might get used to it."

"He wouldn't want that, that's for sure," I say. "Not with Rosemary coming back in two weeks."

There's a brief look of hurt in his face, and I wonder what it would be like to reach over the table and touch him. I am thinking that he does not want this to go on, and I know what he is asking me to do. I know what he is afraid to ask me to do, and I reach my hand into my pocket and feel the keys there like a charm.

"I understand how you feel."

"How could you possibly understand?" he asks, as though he's the most miserable person alive.

Tonight I saw Ray and Lawrence go to the Bijou for a screening of Fassbinder's *In the Year of Thirteen Moons*. If I could have, I would have warned them about it. I don't know how they could sit through that movie without feeling very uncomfortable; the lead character has a sex change to satisfy a rich, straight man who doesn't care about her. It's no wonder she tells her life story in a slaughterhouse.

It helps to know where they are and how long they'll be gone. I could probably turn on the lights. But I know this house by heart already, and besides, I like the feeling of being a shadow here, keeping away from the windows, touching everything with these gloves, Rosemary's gloves which I'm now sure I made the right decision in taking the first night I came here.

There are two places I always have to check for clues: the bedroom and the nursery. I don't know what it is that I'm looking for. I guess I'm just interested in whatever it is they leave behind. I've felt compelled to take only a few things out of here, but they are inexplicable treasures to me.

At first, I touch the heavy draperies on the windows, the thick spreads on the bed. Then, like a neoclassical bedroom to which the wicked son is always returning, I sit on the edge of the bed and draw the cold, white sheets up to my face, with more than a sense of ownership. It really is, for a moment, like I've entered a painting, feeling so completely where I should be, as though I were positioned there by an artist.

Ray and Lawrence would feel it too, the limiting, perfecting structure of our interaction.

It was no surprise when Lawrence, five days before Rosemary's return, called to inform me that Ray had asked him not to stay at the house any longer. Time itself was conspiring to that end, but I was surprised by Lawrence's breathless weeping which made it hard to comfort him. I asked him over.

I look around the apartment and it seems as though I have moved in at last. The boxes are unpacked; some of my favorite postcards are taped to the wall behind my desk. I've taken down the mirror tiles and stacked them inside the closet. The room and the fixtures themselves are ugly, but there is the feeling that someone lives here now, that someone is making do.

When Lawrence arrives, he concurs. "I feel more at home here than even at my own apartment," he says. He looks exhausted.

"Well, I guess so," I say. "Ray pays your rent."

He sits there drinking, silent.

"I don't know what happened," Lawrence says. "He started accusing me of things that I don't know anything about. Little things were missing, that he couldn't turn up—some of Rosemary's jewelry, which I'd never take." He looks so humiliated, as though he is accusing himself.

"Why would he think you did that?" I ask him.

"I don't know," he says angrily. "But he kept asking me if I was angry about Rosemary, and how I felt about them having a baby. I told him none of that mattered, and it didn't. But I think Rosemary took those things with her, or nothing's really gone and he's just finding a way to get rid of me."

"Maybe he doesn't find you compatible with his new family?"

"I didn't ask to stay at his house," Lawrence says. "I would have been content to have kept things the way they were."

"Well, that's how things are now, right? Back to the way they were?"

"No," he says. "He hates me now. He's politely asked me out of his life. Not even politely."

"He's afraid of you."

"I don't know why he thinks I would ever steal from him or try to disrupt his family."

"That comes with being the lover on the side," I remind him.

I don't know which one of us introduced the idea of mischief. Our desires seemed to cross then and run concurrently. By the end of the evening, we were sitting on the floor with a bottle of wine between us, laughing and crying, imagining ways to terrorize Ray.

"Let's make a baby," I suggest. I am thinking of the boxed baby clothes and the baby bounce swing I have in my closet.

"What are you talking about?" he asks.

"I found these baby clothes at the Salvation Army drop box. I can't imagine what else to do with them but make a little baby for him. It will be the one you couldn't have."

"Rosemary's Baby!" he shouts. We both roar.

We tear the plastic wrap from the boxes. On the collar of the little pink nightie Lawrence writes "Rosemary's Baby" in black magic marker. We stuff the clothes with an old gray pillow, leaving it bursting from the collar as a head. I draw in two weeping eyes.

I think how excited Ray must be about his family's return. He has come so far with the nursery. The wallpaper has cheery yellow balloons; the seams are perfect. The whole house smells like glue.

I wonder how he will feel about these stolen baby clothes showing up again.

Lawrence is busy drawing in the mouth.

"Cut it in," I say, our prank becoming a mad kind of voodoo. I hand him a knife I'd lifted.

He cuts through the pillowcase and pulls the dirty stuffing up out of the lips.

"Let's make them red," he suggests.

I don't have any paint, so we stain them with Mercurochrome.

Lawrence suggests we keep the knife buried in its head. We sit it up in the bounce swing like that. We hang it from a nail and stare at it. I force myself to laugh at its ugliness. Lawrence can't.

"Maybe we shouldn't," he murmurs.

"What did you expect? The Hardy Boys?"

"But I care about him," he says, confused.

"There'll be others."

"I don't think you understand the way I feel. I don't think you could understand it."

"No," I say. "Probably not. It's too subtle for me." And I begin to think how they tried to make me beautiful, how anything attractive in my face was put there by the doctors. They really wrestled it out of me, extracted it, but at such high cost and such great pain.

"I want to understand," I tell Lawrence.

They laid me on the table and gave me two rubber balls to squeeze. They were chewed up with nail marks. I rotated them slowly.

A German nurse with soft blonde hair dried her hands of sterilizing liquid. She directed my father, "Will you please hold your son's legs."

I felt his hands loosely holding my ankles. He looked at me, miserable. My mother stood small in the doorway.

The nurse lowered a bright light over my face. I looked into it. At first there was nothing but whiteness. Then I saw an eyeball floating between two lights.

"This is a magnifying lamp," the nurse explained. I saw the eye blink on the other side.

I imagined what she was seeing: the cores of blackheads, a violent chemistry in the cyst, here and there a black whisker shockingly cutting its way through the thick skin.

I saw the doctor enter through the glow of the light, radiant, drawing a rubber glove over one hand. In the other he held a needle. He pushed the sweaty hair off my forehead and began pressing the cysts along my cheek.

He worked silently.

Finally he said, "This will hurt. But when you're well, you will thank me." I saw the nurse nodding, reverent.

With the first prick, blood flashed across the dull green wall. My nails sank into the red balls. I felt his fingers pressing down the boil.

"It is the problem of evil," I thought I heard the doctor say.

I remembered the video we all had to watch in the crowded lobby. The doctor's only child born with cystic acne all over its innocent body. The German doctor mournfully narrated, "My wife and I wept when our child was born to us with cystic acne. He screamed constantly as an infant, unable to lie in one position for very long."

Hundreds of before-and-after photos of patients were flashed on the screen while the doctor talked his theory of enzymic reactions, postules, scarring. Everyone was standing around the TV with their arms folded over their chests; they were secretly looking at the faces of the others, measuring the severity of their problem against everyone else's condition.

I remember staring constantly at a mirror. For me, the mirror was like skin, always healing itself, always getting better. Though I wanted nothing but the truth about my face, the mirror could never reflect it accurately; I saw only the desperate effort to heal.

My eyes were searching the doctor's. He was the only one who saw my condition the way I did, and he was punishing me for it. I saw my blood arc across his coat. He did not stop at my weeping. He did not hear my screaming. If he heard it, it was a tiny scream; I sounded like an infant to him. He would have strangled me if I didn't bear that resemblance to his son.

The nurse saw I was about to pass out. Perhaps she heard it in my breathing. If there was a soul in there, I physically forced it out.

The doctor peeled his glove off. As I slowly began to sit up on the table, an assistant entered the room and snapped a Polaroid.

There is a light drizzle, so we put the baby, swing and all, into a plastic garbage bag, and carry it to the house. I make Lawrence carry it, it's his gesture.

I stand up in the park, behind the oak tree where I'd first seen Ray's home. We both wear ski masks. Before Lawrence takes the baby down to the house, we look at each other, and it seems that for the first time we can really see each other, desperate eyes and faces sheathed in wool. The drizzle persists. I wish I could feel it on my face, but this mask lets nothing through.

I watch Lawrence furtively make his way up to the door, strip off the garbage bag, and hang the baby up under the porch light. It swings eerily and misshapen as Lawrence comes off the porch.

We stare at it from the park.

"Let's get out of here. Let's go to my studio."

When we enter his studio, he grabs both my hands. "Can you believe how that thing looked?" he asks excitedly.

"So beautiful," I assure him, "his beautiful little baby."

Lawrence puts up tea. While I sip it, I think about Lawrence staying here until he finds another place. It is small and smells like paint, and it's cold, but nothing a space heater couldn't improve. I would put him up too, if it comes to that.

Suddenly, there is an oppressive weight all around us, as though the walls of the studio are closing in, and I notice we are sitting, facing one another, our knees touching. Lawrence's face is twisted with confused sadness. Maybe it's our touching, our close proximity, that enables me to feel it, too.

"He'll know it was me?" he asks, as though everything had suddenly dawned on him.

I feel his tearful shaking rising up from my knees, like we are two old trees that have grown together.

"How will I ever explain it to him?" he asks, clutching me.

And though I know it will never suffice, I draw him close and forgive him.

Keloid

The bodies came together, separated, reconnected with others. Alan and I were both distracted. We watched, looked at each other, watched again. We moved closer to each other until our arms touched. That's all it takes, usually, to move you from spectator to participant. When he brought a beer to his mouth, I ventured to look at his face: dark rings around his eyes, prominent nose, goatee. He reached over and felt my dick. It was hard, but I took his hand away from it. I walked toward a covered pool table and sat down on it. He followed. "Did you want me to join you?" he asked.

"Yes," I answered, "but I didn't like standing there. I felt I was on the edge of something."

"You don't like that feeling?"

"I used to."

He reached for me again, kissed me this time. I savored

the taste of beer on his lips. I was a recovering ex-junkie, coming up on a first birthday without drug or drink. Or sex. The kiss felt familiar and dangerous. "I prefer equilibrium now," I told him.

We started to talk about the bar, then about the sex going on across the room. "I'm amazed they let this go on," he said. "But then prohibition didn't stop drinking."

"It's almost mundane though, don't you think?" I asked. "This kind of backroom sex doesn't seem as celebratory or radical as I used to think."

"So, what brings you here?" He kept his hand on my leg.

"Habit," I answered, and the word saddened me for a moment. "And I was looking for something unusual, like conversation."

"Let's steer away from the confessional," he said. "I'm a psychiatrist, and I'm not working until Monday."

"What's not confessional?" I asked. "Lies?"

"Stories."

I begin to tell him one I remember reading as a child, without recalling its origins and freely embellishing its simple plot:

"A man wanders through a strange town. Everyone he meets tells him he better get himself indoors before sundown. He wanders from place to place but can't find a room. He finally finds a large, old-fashioned supper club, someplace like after World War II, where there's music, old music—you know how creepy nostalgia is—and a lot of couples in formal wear in arched, almost positioned situations," I looked at Alan, smiling patiently despite the jostling of the club around us. "The man makes his way to a table and sits alone. He notices the heavy, burgundy velvet theatre curtains covering the walls. No wonder the place feels so muted. The people around him are discreet, formal even."

Alan interjected, "They're not discreet here." He looked over his shoulder where inky black shadows amassed in a corner. We both watched long enough and in silence, until we could make out a pale boy at the back of the bar and the numerous hands running over him, obsessional, either building him from nothing or taking pieces of him away.

I went on with this story: "He senses something—a lack of eye contact, an almost chilling sense of personal space. The waiter arrives at his table, and comments with disinterest, 'You haven't been here before,' while placing a glass of red wine before him. The man says, 'You must be mistaken, I don't drink alcohol,' and looks around to see who might have ordered it for him. 'It will warm you,' the waiter laughs like Richard Widmark, whom he resembles. He turns away from him like all the other eyes.

"The man looks at the glass of wine before him and he knows that this glass contains his past and his future. Maybe he sees himself leaving his wife and family, losing everything in seeking out its one spectacular comfort. It is probably what brought him here, to this place where nobody looks at him.

"He thinks, the waiter is right, it's the only thing that warms me, and his hand reaches for it with the heaviness that is supposed to be something of the heart, and he puts it to his lips."

Alan raised his bottle as though in a toast. He toasted without me because I was not drinking. I noticed Alan's eyes seeking out the boy at the back of the bar, now completely naked, languishing in the arms of three leather-clad men. I continued, "The drink strangely fortifies him; he feels more *himself* than he ever has. He empties the glass quickly and asks the waiter for more—for a carafe. He drinks until he's happy to be left alone, to be at the center of a room full of people gathered away from him, watching him with less discretion now. The waiter has placed a second and third carafe on the table. He drinks because he's hungry, alone, tired, without accommodation, without wife, faith, ambition. The people he sees from the corner of his eyes are raising glasses, empty glasses in his honor. They draw the curtains back on mirrored walls in which the whole room is dizzyingly reproduced. It takes a moment before he realizes he is the only person reflected in the mirrors. The imperious others stand not far from him, now openly watching him. 'Fuck off,' he says to them, raising his own empty glass and tossing it at the mirror before blacking out.

"When he awakens, his head pounds more fiercely than from a normal hangover and his throat is aching. He looks down the length of his body, his head weakly turning upwards to glimpse his feet. He realizes he is hanging, naked, upside down from a noose burning his ankles. He sees it in the mirror suddenly—a tap implanted in his throat. He is unable to see the reflectionless guests who gather around him with their glasses full, closing in on him. He wants to scream but feels the pressure of someone's finger on the tap, filling their glass with the silent, inarticulate draft of his life."

"No one's ever tried to seduce me with a vampire story," Alan said, leaning over me and pressing his lips, his teeth against my throat. I didn't resist him. The movement of his hands on my bare arms brought me back to my own body, without the fear and distrust of pleasure my addiction had taught me.

"I'm Adam," I said, which in a place like this is offering up a lot. I wanted to do it, if only to differentiate myself from the man in my story, who's content to be alone, isolated even from his past. I don't like my own, but I feel crippled somehow without it. "Telling you about me would probably have been less confessional," I assured him.

"It's not that I don't want to know about you—"

"I'm a heroin addict with ten months clean," I told him. "Does that bother you?"

He asked me if I'd shared needles, and I explained I'd begun using after I'd heard about AIDS, and never took that risk. I told him I was negative, a fact I'd discovered through the mandatory testing that was part of a drug study protocol at UC. I told him I'd finally gotten my libido back, with a vengeance.

"I see," he said, his hand disappearing into my opened pants.

I'd had some rough years, but I wanted him to believe I wasn't that person anymore, and invited him home to meet the person I'd become.

The activity in the bar had a strange pull over us; we kept looking back as though we'd left something behind.

Once home, he directed his attention toward the artwork on my walls. He stood scrutinizing an unframed Joel Peter Witkin photograph, *Penitente*, in which my friend Eric is crucified between two monkeys, also stretched on crosses. They all bare numbers on their chests.

"Was he really crucified?"

I recognized his perversity, a shared prurience. Relationships are built on so much less, I thought.

"He was a masochist and an exhibitionist; he had all the saintly attributes." I remembered one night when Eric arrived at my door in his drag persona, Jayne Mansonfield, tottering on a broken heel and wearing a soft suitcase on her head she'd modeled like a beret. I couldn't imagine how she made the bus ride without being harrassed. I'd always done drag with others and here she was alone and not exactly passing. She was part of a performance group that did body manipulations. She seemed sort of dazed at the doorway after a performance in which they'd taken a chunk of skin from the center of her chest with an exacto knife; then packed it with ash. A *keloid*, she called it. I realized when she opened her blouse to show off her wound what she'd used to keep potential antagonists at bay. I could imagine her swaggering through the bus, exposing the hole they'd gouged, created just for its healing, like the upraised scars that pattern the backs of certain tribal peoples.

"Jayne was my protector on the streets of the Tenderloin," I told Alan, "She wasn't only tough in her performances. I remember her threatening a gang who'd circled us, reaching for our skirts, and calling us men—the most stinging and ignorant comment you can make to a drag queen. Her heel was off in no time. She threatened the most belligerent of the group, insisting she was going to take some brain home on her heel—and she would have, had she needed to."

Alan looked closer at the photograph, the body bowing out from the cross. I assumed he was looking at the feet where the spike was driven, but he turned to me and said, "Not a bad cock."

The keloid—which never completely healed while she was alive—came to resemble the KS that toughened her skin and swarmed her internal organs. "I've always had to push my body," she wrote, "test it's capacity to heal." Her doctors provided new ways for her to test her body—ways that rivaled the witches' cradles and suspension hooks of her performance troupe. She went from heavy doses of AZT to interferon. She said she could always feel the chemotherapy burning beneath her keloid.

She wrote letters from home, a place that had never been her home before, one of her mother's degraded properties in Albuquerque. She'd described it as a "shit-encrusted, three-floor basement." She got sicker and it didn't seem to matter as much. "My home is in my body," she wrote, "and I've never rested there."

I didn't write back. I kept her letters by my bed, and read them when I was high so the words had no voice attached, just text that could have been written by anyone, a kind of ephemera, coaxing only a memory of her—as though she'd already been buried.

I didn't tell Alan that I'd once left San Francisco in an effort to get away from AIDS. Jayne left after a series of inner ear infections so disabling she was fired from her bakery job and evicted from her apartment. That's how I got the photograph, no doubt worth a great deal in a gallery. I think I bought it for a hundred dollars. Jayne used the money for an emergency plane ticket.

Maybe I wanted to leave San Francisco because no one was dying quietly or courageously in clean hospitals with attendants to apologize for their anger, to explain their irritability, or just to take care of them. My friends were dying in squalor and addiction, and I kept thinking, "Where is the romantic San Francisco of Hitchcock's *Vertigo*?" After a year, I returned to San Francisco, fortified. I expected AIDS. I didn't expect heroin, the shooting galleries, the casualties of addiction, those slow deaths, that particular dementia.

"I'll be speaking at an American Physicians for Human Rights conference on Monday, then it's back home to New York," Alan said, stepping out of his shoes and dropping onto my battered sectional. He seemed surprisingly not worried about his presentation, not pressed to prepare, and I thought of that as one of the first differences between us I should take note of and learn from. Without knowing the content of his speech or even the parameters of his scientific specialty, I'd taken him as a mentor.

"How did you get into AIDS Psychobiology?" I asked, sitting beside him.

"I was working in a gay men's health clinic at the start of a major hepatitis C study. Later I began a protocol involving two of the hottest drugs on the market, AZT and Prozac. In every situation, putting two and two together amounted to more than I'd bargained for."

"Well, that's something this disease has taught us," I said, thinking casualties, not careers.

Alan said he remembered small articles in the paper, the nameless gay cancer, treating the confusion and indignance around the sarcoma or swollen lymph. There were tricyclics, answers. His research suddenly timely: the interaction of antidepressants with AZT, the effects of grieving, relapse into unsafe practices, the reluctance of disclosing HIV status. He initiated protocols almost a decade ago still being re-created with modest changes in the variables today. There was no escaping it, AIDS or death, so easily equated early on. There was only escalation, data, statistics. Opportunities, too.

He began to unbutton his shirt, and I went into the kitchen and brought out a bottle of Calistoga and two glasses. He called after me, "I've got a party to attend tomorrow. I'd like you to come. I can't promise it'll be interesting, though."

"What kind of party?" I asked.

"Mostly doctors and researchers. Some of the big ones: Conant, Volberding, Don Abrams..."

The names were familiar. I knew they were the so-called leaders in the fight against AIDS, but I had little knowledge of their work, or the media surrounding it. The unshakable junkie in me was already intimidated. I imagined myself like a page from *Gray's Anatomy* where every damaged vein and floating organ would be observed. I told myself that it wouldn't be me they objected to, but the fact that I didn't know who they were, let alone understand or value their research. Nonetheless, it was a world I found intriguing, and, I imagined, not overtly hostile. A raised eyebrow here and there was nothing compared to the company I'd found in shooting galleries in the Mission.

"I'll go," I said.

We made love like survivors, without the fears and petty encumbrances that might have made us afraid of deep kisses. I treat everyone as though they're positive, so I needn't ask and they don't have to tell. This approach was my fortification upon returning to San Francisco, this, and, of course, thc testing that was part of the drug study. I had six AIDS tests and came up negative each time. Each time I feared and doubted the results. I could always seroconvert. Safe sex was still a personal thing, each person with his own idea of what it meant. My formulations were simple—one thing I remembered from a science class was that *science loves the simplest solution*, something I no longer take for granted. I decided to make simple changes: no unprotected anal sex, no swallowing semen.

Alan slipped to his knees in my living room. He unbuttoned his own pants while he sucked me with abandon, glancing up at me as though desiring instruction—which I offered. He was wearing the Versace suit he'd worn earlier to a benefit. It was clear this was how he wanted to get off, sucking me while I bent over him, forcing myself down his throat. I told him I was going to cum. When I orgasmed he swallowed hungrily and came himself. I was more amused than surprised by the irony. Doctors are people after all, and no one who gives advice lives by it, at least as far as I can tell. But Alan assured me swallowing semen was reasonably safe, citing the stomach acid argument. Everyone nowadays seems to have perfected their justifications for the acts they prefer engaging in—those that are possibly unsafe seem to bear a benign warning, like the surgeon general's on a pack of cigarettes. "I'm negative," I told him, "so you can drink as much as you can draw and no apologies."

But something about our sex didn't sit right with me. Somehow I'd forgotten my fears of seroconversion while ejaculating into his willing and appreciative throat. Nothing, however, indicated Alan suffered any reservations. There's a kind of certainty about our individually accepted safe-sex parameters. The problem is meeting someone whose parameters are wider than yours. This, of course, could apply to any ethical concern, to any ideology. The more you encompass, the less adjustment you need to make.

I put it out of my mind, and hung his clothes as he stepped out of them. He lay on my mattress on the floor, and I put on a tape. He'd brought a small toiletries bag, and arranged a number of prescription bottles on the carpet. They looked like brown colums. "Is that your model of the Parthenon, or the design for a new NIH?" I asked.

"The Ritalin is for my attention deficit disorder, Elavil for depression, and this," he said, dropping two pills into his palm, "is Halcyon—for a good night's sleep in a strange place."

"I guess you have no reason to shudder at my heroin addiction," I said.

He swallowed the pills with the Calistoga; then opened his briefcase and drew out a paper by a colleague of his we'd be meeting the following morning for breakfast. I liked his willingness to include me in his life—the simple but comprehensive acceptance he had of mine.

The paper was a statistical evaluation of the rate of HIV transmission in three artificially distinguished groups: call boys, street hustlers, and those who worked with escort services. While I read the researcher's specifics for each category, I found myself becoming more and more exasperated with the paper. It seemed to have no ultimate aim beyond its tabulations and tables—the boys were already lost to this researcher; they'd become the raw data of their acts, desperate or otherwise.

"I don't know," I said. "I believe in good old intervention."

"Well," Alan answered, "how do you design a good intervention plan without the necessary data?"

"When someone's hit by a car, you don't design a study to get them out of the road."

But reaction to this disease wasn't about haste anymore; it wasn't about responding to an emergency. Now it was about design and implementation, competitive proposals and salaries. The escalating numbers were not emergencies, but time lines and spreadsheets.

The way my friends had described AZT to me, it reminded me of methadone maintenance: methadone keeps junkies sick and dependent on the government; AZT keeps people sick and dependent on the pharmaceutical companies. I didn't want to sound cynical, but I suppose I was. It seemed simple minded, like conspiracy theory or something, and I'd always liked complexity, something more challenging than greed, or sloth, or wastefulness, or just plain ineptitude.

The next morning we had breakfast with the "call boys' researcher," someone I had hoped might show signs of a previous history as one, or a pervert obsessed with them. His home was near the top of Twin Peaks, unassuming from the outside, but with a sprawling and impeccably designed interior. He was obviously proud of the place, judging by the sweeping hand gesture he used to welcome us inside. He eyed me without the slightest discretion, and I eyed him back. He was middle-aged, with a face that presented no disturbing or extraordinary features, like the strain of genius, or even ordinary struggle. It was a full and contented face, and the body seemed to match, buffed but not lean, mostly genetic mass and little work. Alan had described him as a "knockout." He guided us through a large sunken living room with its smart leather couch and track lighting aimed upon the framed international safe sex posters, some quite risqué for a room as tidy as this was, and one which showcased the most benign treasures: a vast fish tank with its solitary puffer and sunken Japanese garden, a cabinet displaying china. We walked up the steps to the kitchen where we met Ken's domestic partner, aproned and busy at work like a simple domestic.

"This is Danny," Ken said, introducing us. "And your name again?"

"Adam," I answered.

"Where'd you meet Alan?" Danny asked, a quizzical look on his face that might have been dull-wittedness.

"In a back room," I answered, before Alan squeezed my arm.

"Well, we weren't in the back room exactly," he corrected, "but at the back of the bar. Adam was telling me horror stories."

"Did Alan share any of his own?" Danny asked.

"I wouldn't be surprised if several of his horror stories were right there in the bar," Ken said, "and let me guess which one it was...My Place?"

"How'd you know?" I asked, amused but concerned. Alan had told me it was his first time there.

"Alan always has someone new to introduce to us. He has a man in every port," Ken answered. "Every neighborhood's a port."

Danny, watching my face, turned toward the sink and started washing potatoes with a brush.

I went outside where the lovers had built a deck. They'd set a table outside, but the sun was so bright we had to sit with our hands visoring our eyes. The yard was so well kept, the trees so cut back, that there was no shade. They brought out omelets with pancetta, fresh tomatoes from the garden, and jack cheese.

"The hash browns are on their way," Danny said.

Alan lavished praise on the garden, their craftsmanship on the deck, and Danny's breakfast. They'd been friends for years, but we all sat stiffly at the table.

Then Ken said something interesting that troubled me.

"I got incredibly sick in Brazil," he said. "Deathly ill."

He dabbed his mouth with his napkin, "The doctor told me I was going to die. I'm actually surprised I didn't. They moved me from a hospital to a care home run by nuns. A priest presided over me. I think they were ready to bury me in the cemetery out back."

"What was the doctor's diagnosis?" Alan asked.

"Cryptococcus," Ken answered.

"That's horrible," I said. "My friend Eddie died of crypto. How'd you regain your health?"

"I don't know," he said, "maybe the influence of all those nuns." He laughed.

"Well, did you get checked out when you got back to the States?"

"I was fine," he said. "I'm *miraculously* fine."

"Maybe it wasn't crypto after all," Alan suggested.

Danny came out of the kitchen, and the conversation went back to home repairs and garden prospects.

Later that day, as Alan and I prepared ourselves for the APHRA party, I asked him if he didn't think Ken was a little evasive about the crypto.

"He's committed to his research, Adam. I hardly think that's someone in denial about AIDS." Alan looked at me crossly, then leaned forward and kissed me.

"I don't think they liked me much," I said.

"Of course they didn't," he answered, kissing my neck.

I pulled him down to the mattress on my floor. "Everything about my life is amateurish to you, isn't it?" I asked.

"One of these days you'll get it together," he said, opening my pants. While he sucked me, I looked at the white ceiling—a white doctor's coat, a flat hard emptiness.

"Hurry up and get dressed," he said, licking my cum from the corners of his mouth. He looked through my closet and asked, "Do you have anything to wear tonight? It's formal."

"What about a tap in my throat?" I asked, still lying on my back, delirious from the sex, which while quick and mechanical, paradoxically assured me of our intimacy and knowledge of each other.

"They're not vampires," he said. "They're M.D. Ph.D.'s."

I followed him into the bathroom, "I want to know what your friends said about me."

"One of them asked if I was going out with a bag person," he said, lathering his face and talking to my reflection in the mirror.

"Well that just goes to show how removed from the real world these people are. I'm sure they'd shit themselves at the sight of real poverty."

"They *merely* commented," he said. "You shouldn't be surprised about that. You're obsessed with sharing your demons first—you practically demand a reaction to them."

"Are you talking about my behavior with you or with them? I don't remember sharing demons with them, and I don't think their comment has anything to do with my past. It's really just about money, isn't it?"

I thought of how Danny had hung my jacket, beating it out before placing it in the closet.

"Why don't you borrow one of mine," Alan said, pointing to a jacket he'd draped over the bathroom door handle, "and let's drop the subject."

"Fine," I answered, looking at myself in it, remembering

the nice clothes I'd had, but sold for drugs. I could still appreciate beautiful things.

His friend Matt picked us up that night in a rusted VW Bug.

I'd seen Matt before—at the gym and at ACT UP events. He leaned over and kissed Alan deeply, knocking the ancient Woodsy Owl air freshener hanging from the rearview mirror. I could see the red burn on his arm where he'd applied DNCB. He was wearing a tank top that showed off his muscular arms and a perfectly rendered tattoo of Caravaggio's *Medusa*.

"This is the best you could offer me?" He asked. "A quick ride to your dinner party before you're out of here?"

"I tried to call you," Alan said, "but you never called back."

"You know how it is. I have a lover now."

"When don't you?" Alan asked.

"What about you?" Matt asked, turning to look at me for the first time. "Still with Jim?"

"This is Adam," Alan said.

We shook hands. He turned to look ahead and started the car.

"You should tell me what to talk about and what not to talk about, " he said.

"Why?" Alan asked, perturbed. "Talk about whatever you'd like. You do anyway."

"Still with Jim?" he asked again. I felt some relief at hearing the question come back.

"Of course," Alan answered.

Then he asked, "How's the KS?"

"They're treating him with interferon." Alan looked out the window, and his profile was clearly unhappy.

"My CD8s look great," Matt said after a while. "The fatigue isn't nearly as bad."

"The fatigue," Alan groaned.

"How'd you two meet?" I asked, oddly compelled to rescue the situation, and not sure for whom.

"We met at the San Francisco AIDS Conference," Matt explained. "Alan promptly seduced me."

Still seduced? I wanted to ask, but kept silent.

A man in every port; Ken had said it, but it seemed petty. Not knowing who to trust wasn't something new to me; it had become a way of life while I was using. It goes without saying—never trust a junkie. There were little dishonesties. At the time I considered them discrepancies: a little less dope when you halved it, a few extra bucks when you copped for someone who didn't know what you could get it for. Even with Jayne, the photo I'd bought for cheap that I thought I would sell later. Something made me keep it. My friends who were long-term survivors of AIDS insisted that they couldn't trust their doctors, researchers, or the pharmaceutical companies. "Save your own life" was their call to battle; they formed motley coalitions, guerrilla clinics.

Matt embarked on a litany of offenses the medical establishment had committed.

"The research is there," he said of DNCB, "but because it's not patentable, the pharmaceutical companies want nothing to do with it. They disregard therapies that might really prove effective in favor of the long-standing antiviral therapies that limit people's life expectancy."

As if needing to explain Matt's passion, Alan turned to me, "Matt was diagnosed with lymphoma several years ago—and just look at that body now." He put his hand through Matt's curly hair.

"I had a life expectancy of weeks, maybe months. They knocked out my immune system before the cancer with every nucleoside analog produced. And after the chemo I had skin like glass, no hair, no eyebrows, no lip color. I had to paint my face in like a doll and wear a shroud.

"Alan thinks it's funny; he thinks I sprang back to life like a plant cutting. Well, the lymph nodes don't grow back after a biopsy. You're just left with the scars of their invasive curiosity."

"I have nothing but respect for you," Alan said. "If DNCB saved you, then I'm thankful you found it."

"Education saved me, and a lack of trust. What I *don't* understand is why you started AZT in the first place."

Alan didn't respond right away, and when he did it was whispered and accusatory. "Do what's right for you, Matt, and let me make my own decisions."

"Whatever—" Matt said, "you trust your colleagues and I guess that's good. I wish I could—but I love life too much."

"What do you do?" Matt asked, turning his attention to me.

"I'm a student," I lied, "in psychology." I realized I was lying to Alan, as well, who hadn't even gotten around to asking me what I did, probably assuming I earned a paycheck being creative, or arrogant, or in recovery. In his world, people got paid for what they did. I'd been out of work for the past eight months and living on GA. The hustle I'd been respected for as a junkie, looking good enough to stay employed, had run itself out.

"Why psychology?" Matt asked.

"To be quite honest," I answered, "I'm interested in what people are willing to tell me about their lives."

"There are a lot of uninteresting people out there," Alan said. "I hope you're not disappointed."

"The truth is what they don't tell you," Matt added.

Many of the doctors and researchers were at the City Club when we finally arrived, holding up their glasses to Alan as we entered the vaultlike, marble lobby—a toast where those honored weren't provided a drink.

"There's Don and Selma," Alan whispered. "Did you see *And the Band Played On*?"

"No," I answered, "no television."

"Don Francis is played by Matthew Modine and Selma Dritz is played by Lily Tomlin. They're the heroes of the film."

Selma, a short woman with brown eyebrows drawn on and a beige sweater— bearing no resemblance to Lily Tomlin that I could see—reached around Alan's neck and hugged him.

"I saw your movie," he said, "and I thought Lily did a great job. She has your feistiness down. What did you think of it?"

"Well, I liked it," she answered. "But a lot of it never happened—or it happened for Hollywood. I for one would never kiss the owner of the baths."

She smiled at me, so I introduced myself.

"This is your friend?" She deferred to Alan.

"Yes," he answered, "he's a psychiatry resident," embellishing the lie I'd hoped he'd forgotten.

Other doctors converged around us, and spoke of ski trips, research funding, and colleagues who'd died.

They seemed to love the surface of things, talking about who was in, who was out, who was funded, and who wasn't. There was a lot of talk about the movie—almost a nostalgia for the difficulties and horrors it chronicled. The history of the epidemic looked good in its encapsulation, felt finite. And the past seems safe when you haven't a clue to approaching the future. We'd all read about the Berlin conference—the revelations of the Concorde study, not particularly startling, about the ineffectiveness, even danger of early intervention with AZT and other antivirals. The heroes and the newcomers at this gathering all seemed suddenly hopeless to me, and I could recognize it now, from my own addiction. In recovery they say, "*doing the same things over and over hoping for different results*."

Alan asked me to go meet people, work the room—a skill I knew he took seriously. The crowd, almost all men, and almost all doctors and researchers, seemed to coalesce around me. These were men I'd be embarrassed to raise my sleeve for, the veins still reluctant to surface. Alan was gone, but they crowded closer, sensing the outsider. I imagined their derision, like his friends we'd had breakfast with. I imagined myself reduced to the anonymous blood sample of an IV drug user.

I went silently to the bar and ordered a glass of wine, where I struck up conversation with the bartender.

"Not a doctor?" I asked him.

"No," he answered, wiping his forehead with his sleeve. "I'm a bartender."

"An anesthesiologist," I suggested.

"That's one way to look at it," he laughed. "Having a nice time?" he asked. "You look lonely."

"Just thinking," I said. I was staring out at the crowd, as though I were pretending to look for someone. Just then, at the catering trays, I saw Jayne, standing lopsided on her broken heel and filling her plate obliviously. I watched her walking through the crowd, blouse open, and the keloid healed over like a peach pit. She sauntered toward me, unacknowledged by the doctors who seemed to clear a way for her unconsciously.

"This is a great party," she said, putting a deviled egg in her mouth.

"Do you really think so?" I asked. "I'm not really sure we belong."

"We're all connected here," she answered, her mouth full. "*Bloodlines*."

"Your friends wanted me to contribute to your obituary, but I couldn't. It seemed wrong. I wasn't there for you when you needed me."

Her tongue darted from her mouth to catch a piece of egg that fell from her lip to the carpet. She took a portion of her wig and daintily wiped her mouth with it. Her face was pearl white and sloppily made up.

"Mirrors don't work for me anymore," she said, reading my criticism.

"I never wrote you," I said, "I was afraid of you. Not AIDS—but death—how close you lived to it."

"You should eat more," she said. "That jacket's much too big for you. By the way, this thing finally healed." She raised her hand up to touch the protrusion in her chest.

"How long did it take?" I asked.

"Forever," she answered, and clumsily stepped backward into the crowd. Then she was gone and Alan emerged. He asked if I could use another glass of wine.

"I think I'll go home now." I put the glass, still full, on the bar. "You have a set of keys."

His slide carousels, brief case and PowerBook were in the hallway when I arrived, a body of work that, more than research, was divination—requiring our best faith. I wondered what he would speak of in his seminar, what justifications in tables or graphs, what picture of the epidemic he would surmise through all the data and losses.

I hung his jacket, left my clothes in a pile on the floor, and slipped beneath the blanket, naked. I thought of Jayne, of how my living had kept me from her dying; what hatred of my own life had kept me from hers; what self-destruction had kept me from sympathy, from responding to her letters. I looked at his medicines, still lined up by his toiletries bag—gods swallowing their own miracles.

I slept briefly before Alan entered the room in darkness. "Are you awake?"

"Yes," I said, rolling over onto my side to look at him. I noticed the projector in his hand.

"I have to check these for tomorrow. Do you mind?"

He plugged in the projector, and a beam of light created a small rectangular box on the wall. I heard the first slide drop down into the carousel, and he focused a picture that meant nothing to me, some viral activity on a cell, then dropped in a succession of other slides with pie charts and tables labeled: *Depression, Enervation, Negative Affect*. Another table headed by *Acute Psychological Phenomena in People with HIV* included sub-headings: *Fear and Anxiety of Isolation and Rejection, of Infecting Others and Being Infected by Them; Depression Over the Virus Controlling Future Life, Over Limits Imposed by Ill-Health and Rejection by Others, from Self-Blame and Recrimination Over Being Exposed to HIV; Guilt Over Past Lifestyle Exposing One to HIV, Over Possibly Having Unwittingly Infected Others.*

"And here's the final image," he said, dropping the slide. "It's very dramatic, very powerful." The image at the foot of my bed was of the globe encapsulated in the virus, the critical card in his divination, the one that would erase our differences, lift the burden of guilt. He shut the projector light off.

"Are you upset about something?" he asked.

I wanted to say I was sorry to hear about his lover, and felt betrayed he hadn't mentioned his status to me—things, it seemed, that might heal between us if we had forever. Even in recognizing the imperative of honesty, I told him I was only upset about his leaving, how short our time was together.

He undressed and got into bed beside me and held me close to him. He whispered, "I'm sorry. I thought I'd lose you if I told you the truth."

I heard him breathless behind me, as though I had some power with which to punish him, some code by which I could judge him. We are, in the end, small gods to each other in whom redemption and desertion are closely tied.

NOTE: DNCB: Dinitrochlorobenzene, a photo chemical used as a potent topical contact sensitizer. DNCB is used to boost cellular immune response resulting in increased numbers of cytotoxic T lymphocytes and natural killer (NK) cells. When applied to the skin in a small patch, DNCB causes an immune response akin to that seen in people sensitive to poison oak.

Dr. K.

I was working determinations at the unemployment office. During a structured interview I found myself staring at his blunt fingers. He tapped them at the edge of the desk, nervous. His voice was so soft, I was forced to incline myself toward him. This mismatch of troubled speech and the tapping of his fingers distracted me—a difficult simplicity to both gestures, an equal inarticulation. I asked again about his last job—why he'd walked off the jobsite and not returned. To this, he responded, "There just wasn't a point to it."

A week later, he stood behind me at the coffee shop. "Remember me?" he asked, "you denied my claim."

"It wasn't a personal decision," I said. "I'm obligated—"

"You don't have to explain. I've been making some money fixing cars, and I do the swap meet on Sundays."

"Let me buy your coffee," I offered.

He continued talking. "It keeps me busy—that and the house." When I asked for the coffee to go, he asked me if I'd like to look at his truck.

"I'm parked just outside your building."

He wasn't kidding about fixing things; the truck was patched and soldered like an old furnace. He opened the truck door for me, lifting a box marked "Biohazard" from the front seat and placing it in the back. "Hop in." He closed the unpaneled door behind me. The window was down. He asked, "Can we go for a short ride?"

I can usually tell a pick up, but it was tough with him. He had a darkness about him that made an advance seem improbable—*there just wasn't a point to it.* There was something about him, or his isolation, that I was familiar with—a transience, an insubstantiality that reminded me of the men I'd gone home with before I'd settled with Tom. Glimpsing into these men's lives held all the fascination for me of a Diane Arbus photograph. They were shop owners, truckers, fathers, addicts and drifters. I'd sit with them in donut shops and cafeterias, have sex with them in trailers and parks, marvel at their failings, catch them on their way down. Before Tom, I sort of accepted the temporariness of these encounters, and even began to enjoy their brevity. You could share a lot very quickly, or nothing at all.

He waited for me to respond. "Sure," I said, "let's go."

I remembered his name from the paperwork. *Mason, John Mason.*

I watched him walk around the front of the truck; he patted the hood like a service station attendant. The thought occurred to me he might be holding some kind of grudge because of my determination; I wondered if I should be concerned with my safety. At that moment, it was the fact that I would have to trust him that excited me.

He sat behind the wheel. "Where to?" he asked.

"Maybe the park," I suggested. "I've only got about a half hour before my next appointment." The thought of the windowless basement I worked in, the rigid scheduling of people, the rote questions and legal responses I communicate seemed suddenly suffocating. I felt compelled to have this encounter—I imagined myself living by swap meets, keeping old appliances running years past their warranties, possessing a surgeon's hands with parts and wires. A fantasy of brute strength and primitive invention overtook me as we walked into the park.

"Do you like your job?" he asked.

"You're not thinking I took special pleasure in denying your claim?" I asked. It sounded bitter; I could teach him a thing or two about what he and I meant in the scheme of things. He laughed though, and for the first time it occurred to me that we might mean something to each other.

"I'm just curious about what you like to do," he said, before leaning into the water fountain. I thought of William Holden in *Picnic*: the depths of simple men that threaten to drown or liberate us. His hair was black and wavy, dense as sealskin. His eyes seemed to have a perpetual squint—one, he explained, was glass. He turned the handle on the water fountain and drank. His lips were still wet when he looked up. He wiped them with the back of his hand. I noticed the U.S. Navy tattoo on his forearm.

The tattoo reminded me of a dealer I knew. I remembered him cleaning his gun after I'd purchased a gram of heroin. He said, "Don't leave until you've cut me some."

"I don't think so." I said this walking backward out of the hotel room. I never took my eyes off the gun. It had been a test, and I remembered feeling exhilirated and fearless walking away from it.

"I'd like to learn how to shoot."

"You never shot a gun before?" John asked.

"No, never had to."

"That's good," he said. "Be glad for that. I don't know why you'd want to, living in the city."

I hadn't put my finger on the strange rage I'd been feeling, angry about altercations with Tom. Just that morning he threw his pills after me, and I left him in tears.

"The city is the best place to have a gun these days," I said, "and besides, if post office workers can get a little crazy, unemployment workers deserve scheduled holidays for massacres."

"They get all the other holidays," he said. Then looking at my expression added, "Just kidding."

We walked to a bench perched over the San Francisco Bay—outside the park a row of mansions were developed around the same view. I pointed out the old Spreckles mansion that Danielle Steele had acquired and was now living in. Beneath the large, draped windows, cherubs held open folds of cement fabric. I imagined it as the palace outside Florence in *The Decameron*, where the wealthy told delicious stories against death, a reprieve from a landscape of plague. When I imagine cloistering myself, I think more of the movie *Salo*, where Italian fascists exercise the unchecked power of the libertine over a select, abducted group of youths. The abductors, having divested themselves of all but their own law, can only learn from their own cruelty.

But my own escape, for better or worse, was almost impossible to imagine anymore—requiring the kind of wealth I'd never touch in this lifetime, built on tawdry stories and generic endings. Still, I could not take my eyes off that impressive estate as we left the park.

Ever since Tom got sick, I started to feel only his disease could reel me back in, the urgency of his condition was the only thing I could respond to. Tom had a fatherly streak: he'd helped me stay clean, paid for my rehabilitation and continuing therapy. He respected me at my depths, and consoled me through a tenuous period of learning to live without heroin. He'd helped me back to life before he shared with me what he'd accepted as his impending death by AIDS. It was our struggles, our eternal vigilance that came to explain our being with each other. It became a way to explain the attraction to our skeptical friends.

I used to talk about the two of us going to India, but Tom resisted. He didn't like the idea that we'd have to entrust ourselves to strangers for directions, accommodations, well-being. As long as I'd been with Tom, we'd forgotten how to do that. Once he started to get sick, I started to think about others, about the revelations of the hundreds of men before him, and about how our life together was different from that, and how it wasn't.

Complicated men have always disappointed me: an economy to their intelligence where brilliance in one area leaves a deficit in another. I thought of Tom, how he carefully probed and reconfigured me, so that I saw myself as someone responsible: a bureaucrat by day, lover of a dying man by night. It didn't surprise me—this new breed of bureaucrat/caretaker. But I'd come to notice a widening blind spot in myself, a kind of painless execution of duties, and then there were the physical manifestations—a numbness that would spread from my fingers to my chest.

It was easy being with John Mason; I had already failed him by denying his claim. My excuse was legislated. *These limits are imposed on me. He must be used to this.* We sat in his truck in front of my workplace.

"I had a nice time," he said. He leaned over and surprised me by closing my hand in his. "Would you come out to my house on the weekend?"

He wants us to get to know each other—as though anyone has time for this anymore. He tried to explain it. He lived outside the city; he'd like to take me shooting. "I'm not real outgoing. It takes me time to open up."

He had a charm that scared me; like heroin, he exuded a kind of peace approximating death—his whole face conforming to the still, tranquil, blue patience of his glass eye. Tom was there, a sceptered skeleton presiding over death, shaking his pills like an instrument of voodoo. I said yes.

I came home after work and caught myself trying to silence the turn of the key in the lock—a tactic I remembered from childhood, arriving after my parents' proscribed hour. That fatherly streak in Tom had had its effect—I'd gone back to secrecy. They'd warned me of this in my rehab at Saint Mary's—secrecy and isolation were addict behaviors. I was letting myself have just a little.

Though I'd discontinued going to meetings after about a year, I'd convinced Tom to help me pay for psychoanalysis. Freud's Eros and Thanatos instincts were practically a schematic for my life. Above all, I was looking for a transmission of Freud himself; Freud, who had created this artificial relationship, suggesting the minutes of the psychoanalytic hour, and who had come to psychoanalysis by conducting a self-analysis. This was the question I regularly posited to my analyst, Can't I do this on my own? answering, Freud did.

Dr. Klein had mastered the screen—a kind of neutral presence upon which the analysand could direct their love and aggression. I saw fit to withhold payment from her for weeks, even when Tom was paying for them, or I'd demand an explanation of her enormous fee. I would constantly test her, certain and uncertain of the person beneath the ever-patient veneer. She was insufferably reflective. *You don't think you deserve this, do you?*

No one deserves this. But I'd continued seeing her, attracted by the almost inanimate aspect of her personality, the deflecting surface I would later project with Tom, but never master. For me, listening and compassion were merged. I wanted to learn the trick of her disengagement. I assured Tom: analysis would make me stronger for him, a better lover. My therapy eased his mind. He became more cautious of my potential for self-destruction when he got sick—I suppose because I'd asked him to lock his drugs in a cabinet, and to keep count of his syringes.

Dr. Klein had reproached me for not addressing my anger over Tom's dying. *Why should I be angry? If dying is anything like my last OD, and I think it probably is, he's in for the time of his life.*

Yes, but you can't have that experience.

I've already had it.

Tom heard me, slowly emerging from the bathroom with an expression I knew too well—*unwanted discovery*. Perhaps there was a new lesion, a rash. He never spoke of them anymore. "I hope you had a better day than I did."

"I usually do," I answered, sidestepping him and moving into the bedroom. He followed me in, and leaned naked on the chest of drawers. I remember his body of just a year ago, not terribly muscular, but certainly there had been shape to his arms and chest. AZT has rubbed out this history, detaching muscles from the bone so that they hang on him and let the bones express themselves beneath his skin.

Tom was a historian with a particular love of the Elizabethan poets. He taught classes at State until six months ago, when he felt he had to quit. He used to ask his students to record themselves reciting the poetry of Marlowe and Shakespeare. The students' disembodied voices would surround his dark desk until late in the evening. They would stammer on the words, step on the music, but he'd listen patiently to their tapes of Donne's "*First Anniversarie.*" I think of Donne and his idiosyncratic imagery of commingling elements—the blood of lovers mixing in the body of a flea—and how his poems, recited in the terrible earnestness of his students, seemed to articulate the love and dread between Tom and me.

> When I am dead, and Doctors know not why,
> And my friends curiositie
> Will have me cut up to survay each part,
> When they shall finde your Picture in my heart,
> You thinke a sodaine dampe of love
> Will through all their senses move,
> And worke on them as mee, and so preferre
> Your murder to the name of Massacre.

I helped Tom into the bed. "I'm sorry about today," he said. "The medicines make me cranky."

I wondered if I'd ever make love to him again. I leaned over and kissed his mouth, explored it with my tongue. I imagined the inside of his mouth, black and flinty like a mine. I didn't look at the resistance in his eyes, but went about kissing him as though restoring his breathing, doing this to him like an emergency worker. But once I'd let him go, I realized I'd held my breath, afraid to smell or taste him. I felt dirty for wanting, and not wanting him.

I want to die. He always says this, but clings, as though addicted to dying. His prescriptions of Demerol are in a cabinet not far from the bed. I ask if he is in pain.

"I'm losing you," he says hoarsely, "that's painful."

My efforts feel like nothing, because they are efforts. Today his liver is bloated. "Stay off the drip," I suggest.

I can't tell him…

We were driving out of the city to San Carlos where John has a large home. We didn't talk much, it was different than our day at the park, everything tinged with a strange quality of intent, a sexual quality that seemed to concern more than excite us. It was dark and I couldn't see much off the side of the highway.

"How long a drive is it?" I asked.

"Not long. You bored?"

"No," I answered almost determinedly. "I'm glad to get away."

"Good," he said.

John reached over and pulled a flashlight from the glove compartment. He pushed a tape into a deck roughly incised in the dashboard. All music from the sixties, early seventies, the Supremes, the Stones, the Doors—co-opted soundtrack music for Vietnam films.

Someday, we'll be together...

The music had a rich melancholy: I imagined John seeking comfort through heroin and Vietnamese boys on rivers burning like a Coppola set. Static, napalm...the hiss of I love yous taught in the absence of maps, weapons, reason. I imagined him confronting the potentialities of his death, forced to pantomime his fear for a boy whose name he can't pronounce, whose feelings he can't determine.

"This music makes me sad," I tell him, "even when it's hopeful."

"Why?" he asks.

"It makes me think of Vietnam, even though I was just a kid during that time. But somehow, it's the war I'm most intrigued by. Maybe because it was televised—but televised without censoring the ugliness."

"I don't think about that stuff," he said. "I couldn't live if I did."

The Stones' "Gimme Shelter" swarmed the cab, impossible to remove from the green of jungles and camouflage.

"You remind me of my last lover—not in a morbid way—just the opposite. You seem very determined about life."

I didn't know what to say, it was such an odd attribute—the rare and complicated quality of the survivor in me, something mistaken for cold efficiency, untroubled acceptance.

I laughed. "What makes you think that?"

"I don't know. Your getting off heroin, holding a job. I don't take that for granted. You want to live." He's unnecessarily convincing.

He pulled the truck off the side of the road and we rattled across a path of dirt and stones.

"This is Crystal Springs," he said. "People cruise up there sometimes," he pointed at a darker patch. "That's where I met Antonio."

He reached beneath the seat and pulled out an old pillowcase. "I only did this once," he explained. "After he died, I started doing a lot of cocaine, and I was sort of at the end of my wire, and I came out here." He reached into the bag. "I just had, you know, some of his underwear with me, and some pictures of him." He pulled out old T-shirts, jock straps. The smell was so pungent and moldering I sickened. I cranked the window open. I watched him in silence, handling the items, shining the flashlight into the pillowcase, illuminating it from inside like an old skin. I wondered if he was going to perform some masturbatory magic with them. I thought of Tom's clothes.

"I wouldn't keep them," I said.

He looked startled. "No," he said, still looking at them. "It's probably not right." He put them back in the pillowcase, and stuffed them back beneath the seat.

We arrived at his house and pulled into the garage. Along the walls of the garage were tall gray shelving units, stacked with numerous boxes, and all draped with thick plastic tarps. The garage was as orderly as a supermarket; along one wall, an enormous collection of canned goods seemed almost displayed, the labels turned out, attesting to either his military background, or his unemployment.

"We have to be quiet when we go in," he said.

"Why? Is someone here?"

"I don't want to wake the dogs."

He opened a door at the back of the garage, and we took a carpeted stairwell into the house. There were pictures too dark to discern, in overwhelming frames. The silhouettes of the furniture looked almost Jacobean: high-backed chairs with grotesque animal heads, griffins, lions, phoenixes. I wondered if Tom would appreciate this gaudy tribute to his favorite period. What would he think of these lions in their permanent ferocity, or the desk, large as our dining room table with legs thick as Atlas's? I imagined Tom dwarfed by it, unable to pull out its drawers, or push it from the center of this room. We walk up three steps to the master bedroom. *How does he afford this? Some pension? Losing an eye…*

There is a large bed at the center, a dark brown chest of drawers, and a writing desk. The light above, on a dimmer switch, casts faint, gold light.

"Get comfortable," he instructed, looking just the opposite.

I sat at the edge of the bed. John pointed out a hand-tinted photograph in a circular frame above the headboard. I took off my shirt despite the cold. "That's Antonio," he said, as though introducing us. The face is intelligent—dark and pock-marked, with thick, circular glasses that make him appear a scientist or aviator.

"What did he do?" I asked, pulling my pants off.

"A writer." He was standing by the desk, still clothed. He turned to open a drawer, and I worried he might pull out a Bible, or worse, a photo album.

He took out paper folded like a business letter and joined me at the bedside, pulling the chain on a small lamp. I put my arm around him and sat close, reading over the letter as he read it aloud.

Dear Dr. K.,

I've never been one to complain about pain, to acknowledge it, even. There wasn't the place or time for it though there was much of it. My lover tells me that terminal people suffer more from their fear around pain than the pain itself. He talks of pain management like time management, efforts that improve us, make us more efficient and vital. But if this pain could be contained, first to just my body and not my fearful and lamenting mind—if it could be shrunk down to the organs in which it originates, or made distinguishable and discrete like tumors, or lesions—it would still not serve to improve my condition or outcome. From the moment this started three years ago with my first pneumonia, I feel I've been on an expedition from which there is no turning back, like I've entered some dense forest where light can't penetrate. My supplies are cumbersome; nuclear medicines for the retinitis, rolling stands the drip bags hang from. I rely on other senses now, some natural, some implanted, and am as foreign to myself as this terrain. I am a habitat overrun with technologies.

My lover will not assist me, Dr. K., he insists he's in it for the "long haul." Perhaps I've worked too hard to take the terror out of this transformation. I wake up from fevers and describe the perfect beading of perspiration on my body like a suit of gems. I describe my fever dreams as though I've been communicating with God. The dreams bring back friends we've lost, and I think he envies these hallucinations. Because he is negative, he will be our survivor, nursing us through lost faculties and tempers, remembering us with photographs, or by cold absence. Even now he's running food and prescriptions over to our friend, Patrick. He pleads with us not to shut him out, now that we're so close to death. He wants inclusion in a process that often I'm excluded from. I'm only holding on to the parts that aren't being taken away. I've told him, I no longer wish to hold on.

I don't believe in God, Dr. K., but I do believe in angels. The dead surround the dying and bring comfort. My lover leaves the TV on when he leaves the house, and the voices change—no longer bringing game shows and the news, but the words of the dead. I saw you on the television last night, sitting gaunt in a Michigan courtroom. The retinitis has blinded my left eye, so it was difficult to make you out. Your skeletal face gave you an appearance I'm used to—so many of us have shrunken down like that.

I thought you were an angel that would bring relief to my bedside. My lover will not assist me, but you would make it painless and final. I felt your presence beside me, unafraid of my will which, despite my weakness, is still strong.

It is wrong to ask a loved one to take these measures—it's a job for angels.

I look up at the photograph. It is a face capable of those feelings, a poet's face, slim and hawkish and brooding. John refolds the letter, places it on the bedside table.

"Was he angry with me, I mean, do you think he was letting me off the hook?" John asks, already aware of the impotence of an answer.

We are sitting on the bed his lover died in, in a room too cold from the air conditioning. I wonder if I'm the first person he'll sleep with since his lover died. I look again at his lover's photograph: his face with sharp, critical, perhaps criticizing features. John's resistance to participate in his lover's euthanasia expressed a quality I admired: a clinging to the known, perhaps even a fear of hell. My mind raced to pity him, his abandonment. Perhaps there is no landscape free of the plague, it stays with us—like decisions we continue to atone. The dead don't comfort, but condemn. John's lover's mouth is pronouncing his curse while I raise the shirt up over John's head, and kiss the tattoo of Vietnam over his breastbone. We lie beneath the animated photograph in our enviable senses.

John has asked me to stay the weekend, so neither of us are disturbed by the premature dissipation of our passion. We have not removed our underwear; we lie side by side, out of breath, hands clasped between us. I feel we need this touching, but sense it blocked by the letter on the night table, unfolding under the dim lamp as though his lover were rereading it.

I ask John about his lover—not so much out of curiosity, but because he is there, occupying John's mind. "Storytelling," I explain, "is what people do during the plague—they hole up somewhere and have a round table."

"Antonio always wanted to talk," he said. "That's why he wrote, I think. There was never an end to what was on his mind.

"After he killed himself—that's when I found his letter—I just went crazy for a couple of years. Whatever got me through Vietnam, I couldn't find. And I've seen a lot of death. I lost my eye." He turned toward me on the pillow. "But when Tony went, I felt like I went blind. I started using drugs, going out on the weekends and through the week. You asked me why I left my job. I couldn't keep a job. I started having all this unsafe sex, a kind of

Russian roulette y'know? Then last year, I found out I had AIDS. Funny, I felt relieved. I stopped looking for whatever it was I was looking for."

"You felt forgiven?" I ask.

"I just got tired."

He closes his eyes, and I find myself touching him the way I do Tom. Not with dread, but resignation—a tiredness all my own. He is sleeping, or pretending sleep, because he pulls me toward him, muttering words into my chest, and his penis presses hard against my leg. Perhaps he's embarrassed about it. He doesn't remove his underwear.

I start to fall off, but for a few moments feel the narcotic half-sleep where Tom can move freely into my thoughts. We walk through a dirty street strung with lights, in perfect health, and only at the periphery do we notice the thin hands of beggars and their pleading eyes.

I wake up to a wetness on my skin that has also permeated my underwear. The light on the night table is still on. I move away from John's body, the evident source of this sweat—the hair on his body and head are slicked down as though he's showered. The corners of his mouth are white, like a child who's drunk milk before bed. I notice the moisture all the way across the covers and mattress.

I decide to take a cold shower, already wondering whether he'd be offended if I slept on a couch, or even on the floor by the bed. I quietly make my way to the door, and begin walking through the long hallway—my hand gliding lightly over the wall, its numerous frames. What felt solid about the home, its upkeep and abundance, makes it also suspect, fortressed, warred upon. I stumble upon a mounted rack. My hand glides over a long hunter's gun. I draw my hand back, worried I might inadvertently trigger it. I move close to a door slightly ajar, further down the hall.

I hear moaning, at first not different from the hum of air conditioners in the house; then pitched oddly and broken as I approach the door. I look behind me to see if John has awoken. *Perhaps it's his dogs.* I imagine John's lover, Antonio, and mine, Tom. Ghosts, though Tom's living. The pained breathing is louder—I see plastic draperies around a hospital bed, the thin body of a man sleeping beneath a drip bag, the flickering eyelids of his uneasy sleep. I notice the stubble over his sunken cheeks like an etched-in shadow.

I move further down the hallway, find the bathroom, and lock myself behind the door.

The world is full of suffering—we can pretend to help, like Dr. Klein, jotting impeccable notes for herself, or like me, making unemployment determinations, asking questions with answers already weighed and evaluated. Or John, whose empathy or guilt will kill him, thin him out like the specter in the room next door. But in every effort to assist the suffering, there's the safety we're forced to maintain to survive. We're emotionally set apart like dominoes that cannot touch each other should one fall. It is why Antonio sought an intervening angel to assist him in his suicide. Even then, the alarming sense of his aloneness, which necessitated his faith in the first place, was all he could count on. I step into the shower and wash John's sweat off my body.

When I return to the room, cold and naked now, I find John still sleeping, though turned in the bed. I feel exhausted, but at the same time my mind is racing. The light on the night table reminds me of Tom's desk, and I'm struck with a certainty that he has died tonight and has cast his pall over this home. I shut out the light and step back into the bed, my body bringing its own moisture to these sheets. I close my eyes and hear Tom's recitation, binding me to him, as though we've never been bound.

Marke but this flea, and marke in this,
How little that which thou deny'st me is;
It suck'd me first, and now sucks thee,
And in this flea, our two bloods mingled bee;
Thou know'st that this cannot be said
A sinne, nor shame, nor losse of maidenhead,
    Yet this enjoyes before it wooe,
    And pamper'd swells with one blood made of two,
    And this, alas, is more than wee would doe.

John is up, and I wonder if he always wakes this early, or he wants to introduce me to his housemate—first thing.

"I've been cleaning up the guns this morning," he says.

"I met your roommate last night," I answer, lifting myself up on forearms and leaning back against the headboard.

"I didn't hear you get up last night," he says, concerned and lowering himself on the bed. "Did you meet Marcus or Patrick?"

"I just saw one guy through the crack of the door. His breathing caught me off guard."

"That's Pat," he says, "I probably should have told you. I've got a kind of hospice going here—most of the guys who've stayed here have been friends of mine, and I run them back and forth to the hospital, get their medications. Truck's pretty handy—some of these guys have boxloads of medicines."

"I wish you would have told me."

"I wanted to take you away from that," he says sheepishly.

"There's no getting away from *that*."

"You're angry now," he says. "Maybe I shouldn't take you shooting." He's smiling, mischievous.

"I've been angry a long time," I say. "Let's shoot."

He lays a revolver on the bed. "Start with this," he advises. "This is a .38 caliber—not much kickback."

"What was the gun I saw on your wall?" I asked.

"That one out there? That's a 30-30 Winchester—'the gun that won the West.' "

He lays a rifle on the bed, next to the revolver. These two cold instruments of certainty—I try to see them as benign, controllable, but like standing at a high window ledge, I feel powerless before them, as though an accident were inevitable, some instability in me being drawn out, more certain than any protective measures.

"Once you pull the trigger," John says, "you'll know who's in control." He leans forward to gather the guns. We both hear knocking at the open door, and notice Pat standing with a bowl of cereal in his hand.

"Hello," he says, his mouth full.

"Come in," I encourage.

"Thank you," he says. "I'm eating the last of your raisin bran, John."

"If your doctor didn't insist you stay in, I'd force you to replace it immediately."

"Cereal is the best sick food—easy to prepare, and always, somehow, it reminds you of home."

He notices the guns.

"John is going to teach me to shoot."

"I hope you're not planning any vigilante-style justice, after all, it's getting harder and harder to point fingers at anyone *responsible*."

Pat looks John over. He is rolling the guns in a blanket. "I thought GI Joe already fought his war," he says. He looks intently at me. "John never takes me out."

"Not true," he answers from the corner of the room.

"Dying is so limiting," he says. "I have too much strength for it."

"You're not dying," John says, walking up beside him, straightening the smock which nonetheless continues to convey sickness.

"No, you're right. I'm presiding over death," Then, pushing John's hand away, "C'mon, John. Who're you kidding? I don't wear this fashion just because it's *in*."

Pat comes off like a ventriloquist's dummy on death's knee.

"I don't mean to be so dramatic," he explains. "Most people are lucky in that they can forget that life sometimes genuinely warrants our attention."

John says, helping him from the bed, "Sick or not, you're as obsessed with life as you are with opera."

John reads us with his life meter. As long as we respond to its shocks, he's convinced of our will to live. This is what he must have felt about Antonio—his determination to die was read as determination, period; perhaps that's the one thing that kept John alive in Vietnam. Tom's relationship to death is more complicated, shot through with the variables of good days, of enormous gratefulness. Death is a promise. Having been denied so many promises, he's skeptical it will ever come. But I begin to wonder if it is my fear, and not his, that makes his suffering, his saying I want to die, a complicated thing.

The neighborhood streets are quiet. Fog drifts down from the hills and thins out over the pavement.

"Are you unhappy about last night?" he asks.

"Not really," I answer, his gentle concern makes me want him, focuses the emptiness of our sexless evening. I put my head in his lap and he strokes my hair. His touch is almost too gentle—

deathbed touching, an understanding that's come too late for both of us.

"I have to go home tonight," I tell him. "I had a strange feeling last night that Tom was dead—that he waited for the moment I'd left to die."

He doesn't answer, but I see him looking out over the road, and his thoughts are suddenly naked, clear as sun on these mountains. *I should have trusted him...*

He pulls the guns from the back of the truck. "The first shot has no target, just to let you feel the gun." He puts the pistol in my hand, and points his rifle out across a clearing of low shrubs. The mountains in the distance are muted by gray fog. I imagine towers on them, medieval castles.

"Not too high," he says, watching me steady both hands before me, holding the gun out like it was an anxious bird. The tingling comes into my fingers, the numbness I associate with caring for Tom.

He holds the rifle by its checkered gun handle. His initials, JM, are engraved on the barrel. And though he's comfortable cocking it, tilting the barrel up, I think of how this instrument of finality, of exactness and timing, makes no sense in his hands, and how the engraving of Vietnam on his chest seems more appropriate than his initials do on the gun. He pops the bullet into the breach, and in a moment, the deafening trajectory and pungent smell of gunfire overwhelm us. "Now it's your turn," he says.

For a moment, the return of stillness after the blast makes everything mute. Then a hand on mine, thin as gauze, guides the short revolver. It is Tom's hand, I think, locking me in. Perhaps it's Antonio's hand. I pull the trigger, startled by the blast, the kick of the gun. But falling back, I'm held by John, whose fingers, still curled around mine, are warm and real.

India

1.

Before my lover died, Wednesday nights were reserved for cards. He'd pull the folding table from the closet, fill some bowls with candy, and wait for his guests to arrive. They were always prompt. They were cordial with me, even though no place was set for me at the table.

When I first moved in, they all volunteered to show me how to play. My lover offered to play with me as a team, but I refused. I always found cards tedious; they insisted my attitude would change once I participated. For the first few weeks, I'd hover around the table looking at each of their hands, incapable of evaluating them. Don and Rob never did get comfortable with my standing behind them and always pressed their cards to their chests when they felt me approach. I began to stand further and further away from the table.

I suspect they never trusted me; perhaps that's the reason I had them over to see his corpse. No knife wounds or rope burns on his throat, just a look of surprise in his still-open eyes, as though he'd walked in on a party thrown in his honor. He died of pneumonia. There were other complications. He had his arms around me when I heard the death rattle. A few moments later, the coffee pot, set on a timer, began to brew.

I called his friends and sat in the bedroom awaiting them. I was afraid if I left his side he might decompose instantly, that I'd open the door of the bedroom for Don and Rob and all they'd see were wrinkled sheets and bones. He was skinny at the end, but not that bad.

When Don and Rob did arrive, they ran to him as though he'd been waiting. It's funny, I thought, they'd been prompt for all the card games but came too late when it really mattered. I moved off the bed and sat in a chair and listened to them weeping behind me. They were trying to hold his clenched hands.

I wanted them to leave. I never saw them in the apartment except for the once a week they played cards, and I felt suddenly as though I had made a mistake by inviting them over. Would he have wanted his card buddies gathered around him after death? How would they know when it was time to leave without a game played to the end, without a winner?

I wanted a drink, but didn't know if custom frowned upon it. I went to the living room and took a bottle from the bar. I was quiet with the bottle so I didn't have to offer them. I didn't care if it was proper, and I didn't want them to join me.

They came out of the room shortly after I'd drained my glass of Scotch. They came out to console me they said, but I was in wonderful shape compared to them. They sat down on the couch and I stood about as far away from them as I would when they were concealing hands. They asked me to bring them tissues and I brought them a roll of toilet paper. When they realized I wasn't tearful, they stopped offering the paper to me and got hold of themselves.

They started asking me questions about my health and what I planned on doing. I answered everything vaguely, but answers that might have contented my lover brought a look of mistrust into their eyes; then it was time to end our service. They kissed me and asked if I wanted to go to the gay church for more comfort, but I declined. Later that afternoon, I emptied our joint account and had traveler's checks made up. He left no will so I decided to have the body burned. He would have wanted a burial, but it was too costly and I couldn't bear to see his friends again.

All of his family were dead and buried somewhere in the Midwest. Only his senile mother remained in a nursing home in Chicago. I think she was beyond knowing or caring whether her son was dead, but I sent her a card anyway. I didn't tell her who I was or how I knew her son. That wouldn't have been important to her now that he was gone. I don't think he'd ever mentioned me to her before.

The cremation was simple enough. They took the body and exchanged it for an urn containing his ashes. I was not encouraged to watch the procedure. The gentleman on the phone explained that it was best to remember a loved one intact. When I received the ashes there were numerous laws explained to me regarding their disposal. I couldn't simply drop them in the ocean or a public garden. They spoke of his ashes as though they were toxic waste. I was surprised they'd given me the urn at all.

I placed it on the mantle carefully, the way he had arranged everything in that apartment. But I could not escape the feeling that where I'd chosen to place the urn was somewhat arbitrary, that the order he had managed in our life and home was not part of my considerations. I wandered about in his bathrobe, feeling compelled to finish off every bottle of liquor in his cabinets, even the heavy cherry liqueurs. I left the dishes in the sink and on the countertops and began eating from the fine china he had stored away for special occasions. What could be more special than his death? With enough drink in me by two P.M., I would lie down on the big, white couch and sleep without any guilt about the sunlight filling the windows of that apartment.

Four days after the cremation, I sat in the living room thumbing a *National Geographic* when I stumbled upon a pictorial of Banares, India's holy city on the Ganges. Hordes of people and cows were pushing through the tiny streets and down the ghats, and at the water's edge, people anointed themselves, washed their clothes, and drew up water in clay pots to carry home. I carried the magazine into the kitchen with me and kept glancing at the pictures while I prepared lunch. The food was getting moldy, and I was at the last of his china. There were two more bottles of wine, though. I uncorked one of the bottles and began to drink until I felt dizzy enough to seriously contemplate India.

We'd talked of taking a trip together, and he'd started the account. He thought it would make him better to have something to save for. I mentioned India to him; I knew what he'd say. *They're starving there*. He was starving here.

I volunteered to pick up his meds when he was sick the first time. But when it got to be regular I'd stay out longer. I liked walking through the stores, the escalators, the bell that quietly sounded before a page was made over the intercom. It reminded me of walking with my hand in my mother's when I still believed that mannequins were people posing. She'd guide me confidently from department to department, and I followed dreamily beside her. Somehow I'd found my hand clutching a stranger's, a woman just as surprised as I who nervously took me to the information desk and turned me over. A prim, unconcerned woman let me talk over the microphone. My tearful panic made me incomprehensible to her so she let me plead my case directly, thinking rightly that my mother would recognize my cry. She came back for me in no time, admonishing me for having gotten lost while covering my blotchy face with kisses.

He would complain at first. He'd tell me not to feel I had to care for him, that there were volunteers he could call, even Don and Rob would be happy to pick up his meds. But I insisted. Nevertheless, there was always something that got in the way of a prompt delivery, buses would break down, stores would close early and I'd be forced to go elsewhere, old friends would turn up out of the blue. Once, when I came home having forgotten the meds entirely, he was sitting up in a chair, head lolling and his breathing imperceptible. I had him rushed to the hospital in an ambulance. Don and Rob visited him regularly, and sat protectively by his bedside. It shouldn't have surprised me when on Wednesday night they resumed the card game in the hospital, using the rolling tray my lover had been eating his breakfast from. By Friday he was released.

Images of India had already begun to impress themselves on me: the public library was featuring it in a bulletin board display during the last month of my lover's life. At the center of several panels of blue contact paper an image of Kali was tacked, red tongue jutting from a lava black face: an expression of fierce rage mute behind glass in a library display. Around this face, like the petals on a black-eyed Susan, were other Indian pictures: a sadhu buried in the ground, with only his head emerging like a strange vegetable; a marketplace jammed with bicycles; a woman on her rooftop watching the monsoon floods wash her possessions away.

Even though it was three weeks before my flight would leave for Calcutta, only the physical presence of the ticket encouraged me to stagger out from under my lassitude. I kept the ticket in the bedroom dresser, in a drawer where my lover had kept his neatly folded boxers. The underwear I'd dumped into a box, but hadn't found a charity for. Everything would have to go into a box to be reclaimed, repossessed. I lifted the ticket from the drawer whenever I returned to the apartment from an errand—inoculations and passport business. I held the ticket too long; I worried about it. It seemed too insubstantial to me; just paper that could degrade in water. I worried over the red carbon that stained my fingers, that I would somehow lose this destination.

What nagged me were his possessions and his friends who left long messages on our machine, asking, under only the thinnest veil of concern for me, what would become of his VCR, his clothes and his car. After about a week of my not returning their calls their memories of him deepened, and they began to ask for his framed movie posters. Mostly they were interested in the Joan Crawford posters they'd once enviously admired; it was fitting that they were so aggressive over these. But they even asked for his china, which I thought of packing up in its sordid condition and shipping off to them.

I'd arranged to leave in three weeks, but by the last two I could barely stand to enter that apartment; not from any haunting memories of him, but because the place had become so disordered. Somehow I felt responsible for that, for not having maintained what we had tended together. So I stayed late into the night at a bar on the corner, where there was pool and a jukebox, and I could sit stirring my drinks for a long time.

Some of the guys would pull up stools beside me and watch me in the mirror until they felt compelled to ask, What's on your mind? or Are you alright? And then I would tell them that my lover had died, and that I was planning to go to India for an indeterminate amount of time. Why? they would ask, or they'd tell me, They're all very poor there or Isn't it dangerous?

Only one man seemed to understand, a black construction worker named Joshua who thought it sounded exotic and who asked me if I liked dark men. I answered yes, and he moved his stool closer.

I brought him back with me that night. I left the lights off in case he could read me too well by the squalor, the half-packed boxes, the dirty dishes. I dragged him down with me on my lover's bed and I begged him to fuck me. I was holding him, kissing him desperately, as though he were a dream I was trying to remember. I ran my lips and nose up the side of his body, searching out his taste and smell, but he had bathed that night and I couldn't find it strong enough. His tongue entered my mouth as though Kali had broken through the display box glass, forcing her mute fury back into my throat.

He told me he was cold, that I was cold, and that my skinny arms couldn't keep him warm. So I asked him to slip on my lover's robe lying at the foot of the bed. He stood up and drew it over him. I sat up in bed admiring him with that pale silk hanging from his shoulders. My lover's white, slender body seemed as cold and far off as the moonlight in the folds of the sheet. We talked tentatively, as though we only knew each other's language from a book. We only wanted to talk about things we'd done, places we'd lived. That was enough. Both of our lives were full of broken lines, false starts. We didn't ask each other questions about how we'd arrived here, what impulses led us. These were simply choices and decisions that we'd made.

He had a serious, attentive look on his face when he'd listen to me, and then the hunger would just appear behind his eyes. He seemed to know my whole situation intuitively, to adapt to it. He spent my last two weeks in the apartment with me, never questioning the disorder, but hastening it. He left holes in the couch, drunkenly missing the ashtray, open cans on the countertops, and clothes strewn around the floor. He was wearing my lover's clothes, drawing them out of the boxes I couldn't bring myself to seal. He could sense that I wouldn't sell my lover's things, or give them up until I had to. He was taking them off my hands.

Two days before I left I sat beside him on the couch showing him pictures from a library book on India. They were photographs of the monsoons, villages lifted up in the muddy water, and all of India looking like a tide: people in train stations and markets and on narrow streets choked with rickshaws and cows. I stared at the blurred faces moving in one direction, down to the burning ghats of Banares, and I wondered if they shared an inherent persistence toward life. I wondered if I moved amongst them if I would share their destiny.

Joshua helped me pack some of my clothes into a piece of my lover's luggage. "The rest," I told him, "goes to you." He accepted calmly, managing what I knew was an eagerness outweighing gratitude.

I put the car keys and the video club card on the table. "Take what you can use and leave the rest," I told him. "There are boxes in the closet for the TV, the VCR, and the stereo."

"You're really not planning to come back, are you?" he asked.

"There won't be much to come back to, will there?"

"I'll drive you to the airport."

On our last night we celebrated, each of us, our private successes. We were both drunk, talking too loud and too grandly. At one point he whispered he loved me, but when I looked at him curiously, he laughed gently and asked me to flick off the light. He was still smiling at me in the dark; I was already a memory to him. Perhaps that was our greatest success, that we never allowed ourselves to become familiar with each other; we'd mastered the end early on. I urged him to hold me as tightly as he could. I wanted him to fill me the way he had my lover's clothes.

I couldn't sleep that night. I only had a few hours before the flight and I suddenly remembered the urn on the mantle. I felt I couldn't leave it in an apartment that would soon be ransacked, then emptied, then tenanted by a stranger. I felt compelled to dispose of the ashes, but I couldn't imagine how to do it, or a suitable place. I only remembered the places I couldn't do it: the beach, the public garden. I wished I hadn't been left with his ashes. His things could be given away, but not his memory. I carried the urn into the bathroom and shut the door behind me. I poured the ash into my hand; there was a lot of it and pieces of bone, too. I turned the faucet on and watched the ash mix with water, and let it run from my open hand down the drain.

I went back into the bedroom where Joshua was sleeping and got under the covers with him. I wondered what kind of life he would slip into once I had left, and wondered too if I was not the first person to leave him with all my possessions the way my lover had left his to me. Already I'd become a traveler, growing lighter with every box I gave away.

Joshua was in the hall, asking me to hurry. I heard his voice, distant as the future. I was walking backwards through the door, my history in that apartment reassembling itself. I was slipping quietly away from Tom and his friends who were still gathered around that folding table, hiding their winning hands.

2.

I woke up in darkness when the crickets began jumping from the squat toilet. Was it morning or evening? I pulled the rusted chain hanging from the bare bulb overhead and the question no longer concerned me. I turned the shower on and sat beneath it wearing my kurta pajama. It would dry in no time in this heat, murderous heat that made it impossible to escape the long, oppressive days. I was in Calcutta, in a rust-painted cement room with an attached bathroom, and I had been there for weeks.

I hadn't planned to stay in Calcutta, but I'd fallen sick, and the train ride to Banares seemed too long and hot to endure. It seemed, also, that I should wait for an experience, especially since I had no plans or engagements, and my clock was still reading the time of another country. So I walked for a few days, short walks in the oppressive heat, until I began to recognize some of the faces, until one of the child beggars began to wait for me, idling outside the guesthouse gate.

Sometimes he'd walk alongside me, patiently waiting for me to finish a bottle of water. I'd hand him the bottle and he'd run off to exchange it for a rupee. One day I told him I would take him for lunch. He pointed to a nearby restaurant crowded with exhausted-looking men who pounded scrap. They watched us blankly as we entered.

The fussy proprietor hit the serving boy on the back of the head, hustling him over to our table. The tourist was going to get special attention.

They served us rice, dahl, and vegetables on a palm leaf. The proprietor and serving boy hovered over us while we ate. My friend made rapid little gestures at his food, then he'd look at me from eyes that were too dark and serious for his age, and it was hard to see the appreciation in them.

The food was bland. I was picking at the rice with my fingers when the serving boy said something in Hindi and my friend looked up from his food. The serving boy said something else. His eyes narrowed and were angry. An argument ensued. The proprietor jumped in and grabbed my friend by the T-shirt. They ushered him out with tears in his eyes.

When I got up to follow, the proprietor handed me the bill. "This boy is no good," he said. "It is not wise for you to spend time with people like that. If you want to give him a few rupees, that is OK, but you should not bring him around with you."

I took my change and walked onto the street, but the boy was gone. He never returned to the guest house. I had saved seven empty bottles for him.

After that I became ill. I was sure it was the food. The manager at the guesthouse insisted that it was the monsoons which had just begun. "Any hospital you go to will be filled with Indian people with the same problem as you. It does not only affect the tourists." He spoke with a prim, English accent, hurriedly, while flapping the pages of his check-in book. He offered this information as consolation to me.

The shower spray restlessly moved from a weak drizzle to an almost painful blast. The water ran down the toilet at the center of the floor. Sometimes feverish, and watching the water drain down that hole, I'd think, "That's what death is like," Then I'd remember my lover's face, the expression fixed on it at death, and that was all I had to go on, the reason I remembered for being here.

It was then I remembered Sukesh, and the previous night; the memory made me feel anxious and powerless.

He might have been following me for some time. There was nothing awkward in his approach, nothing to suggest spontaneity.

"Excuse me sir, where are you going?"

His voice had such authority that I asked myself if I was lost before I remembered that I was walking without a destination.

I answered, "I was thinking I might have a drink."

"Come along then," he said, touching my sleeve. "There is a place just here on Park Street where you can drink. They also play live music there."

I followed him tentatively. *I must tell him I don't want a guide.* But his face was so beautiful and determined. I thought, I must have a drink with him. His eyes were pulled slightly by his turban, which made them seem hard and judging, but his lips were soft. They were dishonest, lips that could lie to me without the slightest tremble. I imagined the lies he could tell me that could make me feel right about my coming to India, lies that might have erased the heat and cramps, the overwhelming lethargy, as though I was slowly being consumed, a rabbit in a snake's jaws.

The doormen on Park Street wore long turbans and white kurtas and stood like grim sentinels under the gas lamps. The bar he chose had heavy curtains over its walls. We sat at a table not far from the empty stage.

"Why did you come to India?" he asked, looking down at his menu.

I felt I wanted to tell him everything, but found myself empty of words.

"I needed to get away from where I was," I answered moodily.

He called the waiter over and began speaking in Hindi.

"I've ordered whiskey and sodas and some pakoras," he said.

"I guess that sounds all right."

"Are you married?" he asked suddenly.

"No."

"I will marry soon," he said soberly. "I will see a picture of her before the wedding, but she will not know me until the ceremony."

"Do you want to marry?" I asked. I wondered if his English was good enough to sense my attraction to him, the real question I was asking.

"I want to fuck a woman very badly," he whispered. "Is it true that in America this happens all the time before marriage?"

"Yes," I answered, swigging the rough whiskey, feeling dispirited and letting it show, hoping the disappointment in my eyes might at least discourage any further questions about American sexuality. The heavy drapes began to make me feel claustrophobic. I told him to order us another round.

"What do you think of Calcutta?" he asked.

Now that was a civil question. "Well, I think it's very beautiful despite the heat."

He looked at me disapprovingly. "Do you think the beggars are beautiful? Have you seen the slums of Howrah?"

I remembered the restaurant manager who thought I'd overstepped my boundaries by taking that boy to lunch. I'd noticed Indian stratification from the moment I'd arrived. I'd watched two fat women preening on their rickshaw pulled by a barefoot man who couldn't have weighed ninety pounds. They paid him without looking at him.

"Maybe I do see beauty in the beggars," I said angrily, "maybe humiliation is good for the human animal."

I might have gone on, but I worried that he might not understand me, if not my words then perhaps my privileged American viewpoint. And I wanted him to understand me because I suddenly felt very alone, and I would have sacrificed my strong opinions if he had asked me to, because the thought of my room depressed me the way my apartment had.

I drank my other whiskey quickly and stared down at his hands which seemed softer than the look I remembered in his eyes.

"What do you do in America?" he asked. His voice had a tentativeness which touched me.

"Well, let's see, I was somebody's lover and before that I was my parents' son." I looked up at him smiling because my answer amused me when I thought about it, and I knew it would not satisfy him.

He had a beaten expression, as though only Americans could afford to be vague; they speak with the mystery of their money.

Maybe I should have lied and told him how hard I'd worked. By now, I was willing to make a concerted effort for him. I might tell him I was a tax accountant—what I imagined all the bespectacled workers in India's banks to be doing. Honesty was simply out of the question; I felt protective of him.

I hoped sex might make us equals.

"I'd like to walk," I said.

He stood up abruptly and we began to leave. I noticed him watching the stage where the musicians were beginning to assemble.

I paid the man sitting in the cashier's window. Sukesh was standing at the door, looking away.

When we left the restaurant, the street was slick.

"It must have rained while we were inside," he said. "Do you want to walk, or would you rather go back?"

I looked at him. Perhaps I was staring. "Do you want to come back to the guesthouse with me?" My voice sounded obscene, the croaking voice of a man luring a young boy into an arcade booth.

"Indians are not allowed into the guesthouses," he answered.

"Even if you're my guest?"

"This is how they do it in India. They protect the tourist from thieves, from any mistake they might make in their judgment." He smiled ironically, an irony that suggested he was wiser than he'd let on.

He took my arm and we began walking. School Street was unlit and silent except for the turnings of beggars on their mats. We stopped under the branches of a large tree grown over an iron gate. He stood behind me and I felt his face on my neck.

"Do you like this?" he whispered while his hand ran down the back of my pants.

"Yes," I answered, feeling loose in my legs, almost feverish.

Then he patted my ass coolly, and resumed walking.

I stood back for a moment, wondering if he would just walk off. I tried to imagine myself walking home alone, but the anger, the humiliation, the dull cramp was too strong in me. I walked behind him until he turned around and smiled. There was that irony again, but there was something inviting, too. I imagined him thinking, Stupid little tourist, you'll get into trouble this way.

"I'll walk you back," he said. He had spiced betel in his mouth and I could smell it on the rain.

It was not a far walk but the silence between us added blocks to it. At the corner of my street a group of beggars and peddlers came out of the darkness and stood around me with their enamel dishes, shaking one or two coins listlessly.

He dispersed them quickly with some harsh-sounding words. Then he stood there like royalty, undisturbed.

"My name is Sukesh," he said, "would you like to see me again?"

"Yes, I think so."

"Tomorrow night?" he asked, taking hold of my hand again.

"Yes," I said, "I don't have any plans." The word *plans* sounded funny in my mouth, it had the rattle of a single coin in a beggar's dish.

"Ten o'clock. Here, on the corner."

"Yes, that's fine," I said, and we parted.

Later, I pulled my knees up to my stomach and let the thin sheet fall from the cot. I felt too weak to get to the bathroom. Too weak. Surely it hadn't been this way before India, but there had been days when I had no feeling for living. I remembered when my lover was still alive and wanted me to walk with him to watch the sunrise, or sometimes up the hill to the neighborhood store. I guess I felt weak even then, and guilty too, because my lover was watching those sunrises as though they were the very last he'd see, and he wanted to believe that every day was a new beginning. I slept through the messages in the sunrise. For me, it was merely the return of the same day, the slow, protracted, and sometimes painless day I'd spent innumerable hours in before. I always told him it was anemia, and that I'd always required a lot of sleep. But sometimes I thought it was him, drawing everything out of me.

In India I didn't spend a moment without it, the weight of exhaustion in my arms and legs and lungs and brain. It sat inside me like a guest, an incubus.

A young boy was sweeping outside my room. I watched him through the small, screened window. He had his shirt off and was wearing a knotted lungi. He was not muscular, but I loved watching the rippling of his chest and legs as he squatted with his whisk broom. His skin was shiny with perspiration, and in the moonlight it looked like black oil. I felt stronger watching him. Like a machine clicking on, the thought of sex dissipated the cramps and strengthened my resolve to see Sukesh again.

I called out to the boy and he approached my doorway nervously. I propped my head up against the headboard and smiled at him. I could almost feel his dark eyes sweeping over my wet pajama. I felt my penis harden under the wet material, and I opened my legs.

"Sir?" he asked, looking to the floor. I imagined him thinking filthy tourist as his eyes took in the cigarette butts and empty bottles.

"What time is it?" I asked. He told me he thought it was nine.

"May I sweep here?" he asked, squatting reticently by the bedside. I saw him looking in my bag, at my Walkman, and I asked him if he would like to hear it. He took it in his hands and stood up with the headphones on. He stood smiling and listening and turning the recorder over in his hands inquisitively. But when he dropped it accidentally, he was very grave.

I took him by the arm. Nothing is damaged, I assured him. I moved my hand gently down his arm and squeezed his hand. He stepped away from me then, and his eyes were hard and mean, even as he apologized.

I walked slowly, deliberately to the corner. I felt punched in the stomach, that kind of pain. I told myself the cramps will stop; I know the rhythm by now. But there was a pool of light under the lamppost where I imagined myself standing, waiting. I imagined how worn I'd look under that light, how stripped and anxious I'd feel.

There was a blackout then, so common in Calcutta that every vendor had their candles burning, dimly illuminating their folded knees, a brocade stretched across their laps, a stitching hand. There were hundreds of these candles burning, but not one strong enough to connect itself to another; there were only the unrelated and anonymous images of labor stretching out before me.

I stood against a wall, conscious of the sewage that runs alongside these buildings; it flows through the gutters on bath waters. I could feel the heat of people around me. I heard them singing, praying, begging. The thought occurred to me that I would never see him in the darkness, or worse, that I would not recognize him, that he would have undergone some change. I was stricken with the thought that he might have forgotten about me entirely and that he would not come at all.

But someone always comes in India. They can detect when you are alone. I wondered if they were this way with other Indians, or could an Indian spend his life begging for contact?

A legless beggar was moving swiftly over the broken street, carrying his weight on his hands. He reached out and clung to my leg. He grimaced as he spoke. He wanted me to see the wounds on his torso, the results of dragging himself through the streets. "You see it is not easy for me, Baba," he said, "if you need any help, just ask the people here for Hanuman. That is what they call me. They call me the name of the monkey god, because I move on my hands." He turned his hands up to me to inspect. They were raw and black. "Like the bottoms of feet," he laughed.

"Shall we go?" I heard someone ask. It was Sukesh. He gripped my arm and pulled me aside. Hanuman followed until Sukesh smacked him on the back of the head. Then he slunk away.

"You must think we have a very backward country," Sukesh said with a shame as red and complex as his turban.

"No," I answered, "I don't think there is any society without need." But he didn't want to hear this. He walked a little ahead of me, and I thought, he is colder tonight.

"What have you seen in Calcutta?" he asked. I was thankful he spoke. We were both trying not to be strangers.

"I've been sick," I said, "so I haven't seen much. I spent an afternoon at the Ram Krishna mission, I saw the four Jain temples." This is stupid, I thought, I don't want to talk about tourist sites. I stopped talking.

We came out on B.B.D. Bag. It was silent and looked different without its crowds. I began to ask him why the Indians hadn't changed the storefronts to match their businesses.

All over Calcutta, the British business names were still painted on the windows, but of course they were Indian businesses now. The Indians were living there like ghosts. They sold saris from antiquarian bookshops and Indian sweets from British knife shops. And though there were "European Coffee" signs, the Indians sold only Nescafe.

"It couldn't cost that much to change the signs," I said.

"Maybe the Indians are trying to pretend this is still an empire. Or maybe they like to deceive the tourists," he said. I heard him laugh but he wasn't sharing it.

He turned off into an alley and I followed mechanically. He did not turn around to see if I had followed him. We were walking through a maze of streets, littered with garbage and smashed chai cups. There were goats nuzzling each other in the smell of slaughter, and blood in black patches on the ground.

He stopped walking and turned to me. He kept his eye on his zipper as he opened it. "Do you want this?" he asked. I went to him and pressed my lips to his neck. He pushed me down by the top of my head. I felt my foot sink into one of the gutters where the sewerage flowed. He was gruff and impatient with his hands, and wouldn't let me move.

And then there was that moment when my discomfort didn't matter, and only his pleasure did. I no longer cared about the goats' blood that stained the knees of my pajama. There was only my need and his pleasure between us. He slumped over me and for a moment I felt his cheek brush my back. And that was it; he was finished with me.

When I stood up, he looked down at my shoes and the stains on my knees.

"Go get cleaned up," he said, "there is a well over there."

"Which way is my guesthouse?" I asked.

He pointed in the direction we had come from and began walking away from me, tentatively at first, and then with determination. I stayed with the goats for some time, and while I stroked their fur, I could smell their blood in the air.

When I arrived at the guesthouse it was late. They'd locked the door and I stood outside knocking to wake the manager. He was angry and disoriented. "This cannot go on any longer," he said. "If you want to stay out all night you should stay at another guesthouse."

I wanted to defend myself. I'd stayed on for many weeks and this was only the third time I'd arrived after the door was locked. His behavior seemed irrational to me. I had always been prompt with my payments, I certainly wasn't noisy in my room, and as the signs posted in the lobby demanded, I had neither indulged in nor kept drugs in my room.

But looking past the manager into the small office where the cot and the bedrolls for the cleaning staff were set up, I saw the young boy I had seen earlier, the boy who had been sweeping in front of my room. He was standing in the shadows, but I could see the same nervous expression he'd had at my doorway. And then I thought I could feel something conspiratorial between the manager and him. I wondered if he had told, if he had felt me seducing him or just thought there was something depraved in the way I talked to him, or the way I looked at him, or touched his hand.

3.

"Dashashwamed," I said to the skinny boy with the bicycle rickshaw, "Shiva Lodge."

He nodded, smiled, and placed my bag on the seat.

"How much?" I asked.

"Thirty rupees," he said. He was firm in his price. He refused to haggle and I dropped it. We moved out into the traffic with him ringing the little bell on his handlebars. The streets narrowed and the horns and bells of the trucks, auto rickshaws, and pulleys grew more chaotic and threatening. I watched the driver's bare, spindly legs working the pedals, the dirty lungi gathered at his thighs. He turned around as we began coasting down a hill. "Shiva Lodge is full," he said, "I'll take you to another lodge, very nice, very cheap."

"No," I told him, "I'm meeting a friend at Shiva Lodge. Take me there." Of course I had been warned of this. The Sikh on the train had sighed, "Banares—the holy city and the city of cheats. Beware of the commission boys, they will never take you where you want to go."

He slowed the rickshaw and stopped before a large yellow house with white columns. "Shiva Lodge," he said, pointing.

"No, I don't believe you," I said. I had been told that the lodge was on the ghat and the upstairs room looked out on the

Ganges. I saw only dust and traffic and two small children squatting by the side of the house. "I'll check it before I pay you." I started to get up, but he punched the pedals and we were out in the traffic again. He was angry now. Over his shoulder he said, "I will take you to Dashashwamed, then you will have to walk a little way. The streets are too narrow to go by rickshaw."

I said, "Take me as close as you can, walk me to the door, and then I'll pay you."

We came into a circular marketplace with several small alleyways running out of it. Along the roadside hundreds of rickshaw drivers were stretched out in their passenger seats shielded from the sun by torn, brown canopies. We were seized upon by beggars and commission boys doling out business cards. I told my driver to walk with me to the lodge, but he refused. He drew the crowd closer, blending in with them and slipping back into the chaos. I couldn't hear his voice over the others. I threatened that I would not pay him unless he showed me the way to the guesthouse, but the crowd began to jostle us and there was nothing but patience in my driver's smile. So I took my bag, paid him, and he pointed down an alley. "Follow it to the ghat. You won't miss it."

The alleyways connected and broke apart from each other, a labyrinth which narrowed and darkened. There was the heavy scent of cow dung burning under chai pots and the hypnotic ringing of temple bells which seemed to vibrate the stone walls. Those walls seemed to close in until I felt a friction in the passing of veiled women and sadhus, and even from the cows passively eating the flowers off the altars. I felt pursued by a menace darker than these faces shrouded and clustered around me; the threat of God that cramped these streets began to eat away at me, and I thought I'd faint at any moment and it would stop. I leaned against a wall and slid down, weak, and retched between my knees. There was blood in it, and flies swarmed it immediately.

I looked up and a boy was standing before me, thin and dirty, holding his hand out stiffly. “Can I help you stand up?” he asked, a persistence in his voice which nagged me.

“I need to sit for awhile. Go on,” I said, shooing him away with my hand, “I’ll be fine on my own.”

He looked around and reluctantly squatted next to me. “Where are you staying?” he asked.

“I’m looking for Shiva Lodge,” I answered, noticing his knee pressed against my leg, “I can’t find it, damn it.” I sounded angry, expecting resignation. “I’m sick,” I said. “I can’t keep walking around like this.”

That rickshaw driver deserves every miserable minute of his life, I thought. And then I remembered the grief in his face as he rode uphill, the stress in his skinny legs, his wheezing breath, and I felt miserable. I trembled that I had any feeling left.

“I’ll take you there,” he said, pulling me to my feet. I gave him my bag, held his arm, and kept my other hand to the wall. “I know the owner of Shiva Lodge very well. He will try to sell you ganja or charas but don’t buy from him. I give you a better deal. You can see me out here all the time,” he said, walking me through the broken streets.

I stared at the ground. Suddenly they all seemed so ridiculous, trying to sell me, sell me, sell me. I laughed out loud.

“What are you laughing for,” he asked.

“You’re all the same,” I said harshly. “You’ll talk behind your best friend’s back to make a deal. You sell each other.”

“That’s not true,” he said. “I only want to make you the best deal.”

“Take me to Shiva Lodge and I’ll pay you five rupees. That’s all I want from you.”

The owner stood at the door in his underwear, shaking his head sadly and telling me not to pay the boy. “I don’t hire commission boys to bring people to my lodge, but you still end up paying." He led me inside, shouting something in Hindi after the boy. The building was silent, cold, gray. The only warmth came from the corner of the room where his large bed was covered in an intricately patterned bedspread, burgundy and purple. A standing lamp cast a dim light on his chillum and pad on a nearby table.

"This looks quiet," I said, looking up three flights and at the chalky white dome overhead. This looks quiet, my voice echoed down.

"It's very quiet," he said.

"I hear the room at the top has a nice view," I said.

"The choice is yours," he said. "There's no one staying here now."

I liked the place at once. And I liked him. The place seemed impenetrable, like a fortress or a chamber room. I felt I needed to shut things out, and the heavy door closing out the dusty sunlight relaxed me almost immediately. Even my voice, echoing from the dome, secured me.

"I need to sit down," I told him. "I feel weak."

"Relax," he said, drawing up a chair, "The room is twenty rupees a night. Do you smoke?" He put the chillum in his mouth and lit it. The hash smelled sweet and I savored the scent, watching the smoke drift up through the empty guesthouse.

"Yes," I answered, and he passed it to me.

I took the room at the top, and when the large wooden shutters were opened I had an unobstructed view of the Ganges and the pilgrims descending to its edge. Sometimes, the monsoon rains would cool the room and leave the floor around my bed wet, and the moonlight glinting from the floor and the Ganges would connect them so that it seemed I was floating on its slow, gray surface. I remember a dream I had after falling asleep during one of the rains. In it, my bed was a raft on the Ganges and I saw religious people bathing in the waters. The water was silver, like a daguerreotype, or a mirror. And the people were bringing the water up to their faces which would change by that contact, suddenly bearing the immutable expressions of old photographs. I remember putting my legs over the side of the raft and the water not being liquid, but ash. And when I cupped my hands and brought it toward my face, the ash began to separate like mercury, revealing a scalp and teeth. And then my legs were brushed by something and I was certain it was the rest of this body I had in my hands. I woke up sweating and would not let myself fall back to sleep. It was five in the morning when I left the lodge and began walking.

The ghats were silent except for the boatmen calling me down to the water. The sadhus sat meditating under large umbrellas, and from the temples I could hear a singer and the tanpura. I walked to the burning ghats where the cremations were well underway and stood above the bodies being prepared with clarified butter and broken sticks. The men who prepared the bodies and the people who mourned and the others who took pictures were all lost in the smoke and the fires which burned all day. And I remember feeling haunted by a loneliness that made me want to get too close to the body on the pyre, as though I might recognize him.

The lodge owner's name was Bijay and after returning from my walk I was greeted by him, sitting on his bed, in his underwear, and smoking his chillum. I sat down next to him and he began by asking me what I had bought. I showed him the bottles of colored powders the Indians use for puja. "You paid too much," he said. "You can get that for half the price, maybe less." And he began a lament of Banares' hustlers, of the crude tactics of his contemporaries, and he ended by saying, with his hands weakly held in front of himself, "This is my prison and my sanctuary."

He had to stay there and wait for tourists. It was useless to ask him out. So I would always make sure to bring in treats for us, mangoes and pomegranates and the Indian sweets I knew he loved. This would always cheer him, or at least grant him the power to speak dismissively about what he considered a conspiracy on the part of his neighbors and friends to put him out of business.

"Why do you think my lodge is empty," he asked, "when all the others are full? I refuse to pay these commission boys so they refuse to take people here. But it is not just them," he said, both angry and despondent, "it's the neighbors, too, the people I've grown up with. They don't like when I tell the tourists the right price for things. They all own shops, but they make a living by cheating. Once a beautiful Swedish girl stayed here and one afternoon she came back to the lodge with some brocades. She told me she had bought them from Aurobindo De, and I was thrilled because I've known this man my whole life. But I was astonished when she told me how much she'd paid. So we went back to his shop together. He was so angry with me because he lost face, and he kept asking me if I was calling him a cheating man. No, I told him, but you've made a mistake. By the next day, no one in the marketplace would wave to me. They all thought I was having an affair with this Swedish girl. That night they threw trash at my front door. I watched them from her window, friends of my parents, even my friends, throwing their trash at my door."

Sometimes, after we had passed the chillum between us, I would ask him, "What do you need them for?" and he would shrug it off. "I don't need them," he would say. But the silence of the empty lodge would come between us, and when I thought of leaving, and him alone there, I wondered how he'd keep from going mad. Another tourist will stay at his lodge, listen to his stories, and perhaps, like me, take some of his sadness with them when they leave.

I had the fever again. Usually at some point during the day I could get out for an hour or two. Often I had to sit, and I never traveled far from the lodge.

I went to the ghats and sat down. The sun was bleary on the horizon. A boy walked toward me carrying a rolled up mat under his arm. He walked up smiling. He stood behind me and squatted down and I felt his knees in my back. He put his hands around my forehead then, still gripping, drew his hands back across my head, pulling my hair back tightly. "Indian head massage," he whispered in my ear, "twenty rupees." I closed my eyes and let him continue. He pressed at my temples with his palms. The fever made it feel like he was shaping fire in my head. I felt myself sweating and breathing hard. I imagined his mouth on my neck and on my ears while his hands covered my eyes and his fingers pinched my eyelids. And then I let my strength go. His fingers pressed at every indentation of my skull. I felt so weak that it seemed he was holding my head up, that his hands had gotten inside my skull and were opening my eyes up from behind.

I felt his hands on my shoulders and under my arms where my lymph nodes were swollen and painful. "Take off your shirt," he said, but he was already lifting it off. Then he rolled out his mat and laid me down on it. He touched my stomach and I winced with pain. "This is all swollen," he said uncomfortably. "I'm not well," I said, trying to lift my head up to see it.

It looked horrible, frightening. My ribs were sunken in, but my stomach looked massive and painful. I couldn't hold my head up any longer and I let it fall back on the mat. I felt my breathing go dry and wheezing. I felt his fingers on my legs and at my thighs. I felt embarrassed by how sexual I felt, and looked down the steps of the ghat; only the boatmen were out, the sun bleeding over the Ganges. And I looked at his eyes, dark and troubled, and at the thin black hair over his lip. And he was smiling as his hands came to my groin. But I wasn't sure of his smile, if it wasn't the smile of someone who will have their revenge.

He put his hands under my neck and lifted me slowly into a sitting position. "I am finished now," he said, "you must feel better?"

"I feel dizzy," and I gripped his arm.

"Eighty rupees," he said, "for the full body massage."

"Twenty," I said, but I suddenly felt choked, like crying.

"Eighty," he persisted.

"OK, eighty. But please help me," I asked. "I don't think I can get back on my own."

But with the rupees crumpled in his hands, he was gone.

I walked up the steps of the ghat and came to the marketplace, but I was already slumped in exhaustion. I was still haunted by his hands—wherever they had been I ached, like he had brought the sickness up in me. The vendors, just setting up, called me over, someone's hand was on my sleeve, I heard, "My brother's shop." I felt myself being pulled along. I was only seeing the ground, the feet passing, a woman's toe ring, the slime on the stone. I was pulled through the market, but they were forcing me so I pulled away. I imagined my face looked bloodless and terrible like a mask. I no longer saw the man who had entreated me to follow, just the blank expressions of the rushing crowd. They watched me walk up the street, then I fell forward, everything went black, and I hit the stone.

Then it resumed more maddening than ever. I came to, and there was pain, light, and noise. And people standing over me and I didn't want their hands. I was so angry to be back. I pushed the hands away, but I saw it was Bijay. I think I laughed when I saw him. He lifted me up, and I let myself be heavy in his arms.

He tried to carry me to the lodge, but he had to stop. A neighbor stood in her doorway, and he talked to her. She took us to a bed and he put me down. I heard him breathing hard over me. I wanted to reach up and touch him but the woman, standing in the shadow of the door, had her arms folded and watched us impatiently. Bijay was sitting next to me on the bed. "You can relax here for as long as you need," he said. But the woman came closer and talked to him in Hindi, and her expression was reserved and fearful. Even through the fever and the pain in my stomach, I was able to imagine her discomfort. Maybe she felt pressured into this, and worried that if her husband came home he would not understand her charity. Maybe, like the Swedish girl, they had whispered about us. They were superstitious of us.

There were people gathered in her doorway, curious and respectful of the pallor of death on my skin. I told Bijay hoarsely that he could walk me back to the lodge. It did not seem too soon for him, either. The fear I had imagined in the woman by the bedside, I realized, was his too. As he guided me carefully into the daylight, I looked back, and her expression and the expressions of the people massed around her seemed livid and jeering. I imagined them with stones in their hands as I laid my head on Bijay's shoulder.

He carried me up the narrow, stone steps to my room at the top of the lodge. "The light," I murmured, and he closed the shutters. "You must eat only curd and bananas," he said. "Maybe we should have a doctor come." I remember fighting his suggestion. "I don't need a doctor," I said bitterly, "I just need to rest." That's just what I'd told my lover. I didn't want to confirm anything. That's what doctors do, just when you start to live with yourself, with the clock winding down in you, just when you begin to tolerate the pain you've always expected. My lover was under a doctor's care after his first bout with pneumonia; he took the pills that sickened him, and when the veins dropped out they put a catheter in his chest. But he never learned to live again; he just kept the apartment in order, an extension of his body, and talked of going somewhere soon, imagining he was not alone when he came home and saw me sitting at the table, a *penitente*. That is why I say he never knew me, because I wouldn't live that way or die that way.

Bijay asked me how it happened, how I came to be so sick. I told him I had an Indian head massage on the steps of the ghat. I wanted to ascribe my sickness to the boy's hands. That's how it felt.

"How much did you pay?" he asked.

"Eighty rupees for the full body," I told him.

"You paid too much. You could have paid forty rupees for an hour in your own room."

"I don't care about it," I said. "I'm not an Indian, and I've never paid an Indian price for anything."

He frowned at me. "You should care," he said; then he closed the door behind him.

I slept restlessly while the shutters banged. I remember waking up at intervals and the light being different in the room. And then it was extinguished. I felt nauseous and walked to the bathroom. I stood over the squat toilet and liquid, like rusty tap water, began to drain from me. And then the vomiting started, but there was no food to bring up. I felt everything convulsing and couldn't stand anymore. I lay curled on the floor a long time, shivering and dehydrated. I told myself to keep quiet. I was afraid of Bijay, of his concern.

The next morning I heard a rattling at my door, and I lay there watching it, amused, thinking it was Bijay carrying curd, not wanting to wake me. Then it burst open, and a monkey baring its teeth stood aggressively in the doorway, watching me. I sat up, though not quickly, frightened but not wanting to scare it. It shot forward into the room and leapt up on the bedframe. Its face was horrifying and compelling. It reached down near my foot and began gathering the blanket in its hand. It drew the covers slowly off me until I was naked there with it. I watched my heart pounding under the skin, I imagined the animal tearing it out. Maybe I would have screamed for Bijay, but the animal became spooked and darted from the room, the covers dragged over the floor.

"I think it would be better for me in America," Bijay said. "Indians are very nosy, they watch you all the time." For three days I had been in bed and no more active than he. I would watch him from above, lighting his chillum and filling his clay pots with bath water. There was nothing here in his tower of silence, nothing but talks with foreigners he couldn't fully understand and who couldn't understand him. No, it was more than language, but life that kept him apart. Maybe he should have cheated, and kept his Indian friends. Now he was completely alone, as far from India as I was, and no closer to America. "I can do whatever I want," he said, "I am still a bachelor, I have no wife, and no dowries to pay. But what good is freedom in India when everyone is watching you, waiting to see what you will do, what mistakes you will make?"

When I left Shiva Lodge, Bijay asked me for my address in America. He handed me the pad and pen and I wrote the old address mechanically. I wondered if, some months down the line, Joshua would get a letter in some uneven hand saying, I will be in America on such and such a date. But I knew he'd be gone, with everything in the apartment, the very last of it.

4.

I rode first class on the way to Jaipur and the berth was empty for most of the ride. It was too hot, even at night, to use the blankets they supplied. Instead, I took a cotton lungi from my bag and wet it down with water I'd brought from the bathroom, then stretched it over myself and it was cool for a while. I kept the windows open even as we made our way across the desert, and the sand began to cover the floor. Eventually the monotonous sound of the train became secondary to the silence of the desert. It seemed as though the tracks were buried behind us like the bones of an animal. During the day I'd see the women coming off the horizon in their brightly dyed veils carrying stones in wide baskets on their heads. From far off, they appeared like sails, their saris beating in the wind. It seemed impossible that they could find their way to the tracks, to the specific spot where they would lay and break their stones. They made their way through the emptiness, over the hot, white sand, as though it was in them, as though emptiness was what they were most certain of. I imagined myself walking out into the desert. Could I read the lines the wind left in the sand, or the snake tracks one sees in the mornings? I knew for certain I'd be lost in the desert silence. But as I lay there, staring out the window, the landscape seemed more and more familiar, and I felt, for the first time, a connection to India and all its unknowable miles. And I felt an empathy too, for my lover who had died, and for all the others who had glimpsed me like an apparition outside a window, a mirage.

I remembered the way he touched me, his need toward the end, parched, drained of life. I was all of his needs, but unavailable. He'd rub my skin, watching it, as though it always changed. And then the weakness, the fatigue that killed his desire. It happened all at once; the selfishness and insecurity and all the desires they brought up were exterminated. He was just looking up at me then, his eyes taking in the vast, empty space. Me in the chair next to him, but not with him. That's when I tried to talk to him, to make him say my name. But there was no more desire in him. I was rubbing his hands when the heat left him. I could feel him taking me with him. That's what scared me the most, that I would die with him or go on living featureless, insubstantial. I found myself clutching his hands; the room silent as if we'd both stopped breathing.

I let the sand pepper my face. I felt it stinging at the corners of my mouth. The moon had risen, perfectly disclike, and the desert stretched out blue-black in the darkness, like a mirror of space. We traveled three hours before we came to the next village.

There were lights strung in the station, and a rush of faces and hands pressed against the grilled windows of the train. Some were offering food or chai, others just hung to the window, staring, smiling. They seemed hypnotized by these faces moving across the desert. I smiled back at them, their faces glowing under the yellow, swinging illuminations of the lanterns. This stream of faces was a mystery they toiled to keep alive with their endless breaking of stones and shifting of iron.

A young man, an Indian in a western-styled suit, entered my berth. There was a crowd of Indian children outside the window by now, pushing their hands through the bars, talking and laughing excitedly amongst themselves. The man went to the window and shut the glass. "They're laughing at you," he said.

"Why?" I asked, stung immediately.

"They're just children," he said, smiling and sitting across from me. "To them you are something new. And then, of course, you're wearing only that lungi over yourself, and you are covered with sand."

"Here," he said, reaching out with a handkerchief, "to wipe the sand from your eyelashes and your lips."

I began to wipe the sand away, but as if I were a child without any understanding of my face, he came and sat next to me, and took the cloth from me and rubbed my face. He moved that cloth like a sculptor smoothing wet clay. He smiled down at me, his eyes observing and comforting at the same time.

"You have a fever," he said.

"I thought so."

"Do you want chai?" he asked, smiling more comfortably as the train moved out of the yellow, generated light of the station. In the dimness he sat facing me and his eyes were charming.

"No," I answered. "Where are you going?"

"To Jaipur. My family has a business there, gems."

"I'm also going to Jaipur," I told him.

"Did you know it is famous for its gems? Look at my ring. Do you like it?"

"Yes," I said, "but I really don't know anything about gems." I looked out the window. *I don't want to go to your jewelry store.*

"This is a Star of Burma."

"It's pretty," I said. My eyes were on the desert, empty.

"Maybe it's not as beautiful as the stars you're looking at," he said, joining me at the window.

"You can't set them in gold and wear them on your finger," I said somberly.

He laughed, though. I was surprised to hear it and turned to look at his face. His eyes were brown and warm in the shadow, and his lips seemed to anticipate a smile but while I looked on him he did not move, just stared into my eyes as though my sadness had contour or meaning. Before I turned away from him I felt his hand move up my back, and with a gentle but determined force, I felt him draw me toward him.

"Have you taken pleasure with an Indian man before?" he whispered.

"No," I answered. *Taken pleasure*—I smiled.

"In India, we are very discreet about this. There are not many Indians who will tell you they're gay. Most of them will marry."

"Are you married?" I asked him.

"No," he said, "I live alone, a very special privilege. I travel often for the business. My education is European, and my way of life is as European as possible in a place like India. They think of me as a kind of madman for living alone, and I still have to stay with my family at least twice a week to prove to them I haven't forgotten them. India is very old. Her customs are protective."

He patted my knee. There was something fatherly about him, or something childish in me.

"I can't let myself touch you like that on the train," he said, withdrawing suddenly.

"Hold me." I pulled his arm over my shoulder, "like you would a drunken friend, or a friend who's sick."

I stretched my legs out behind him and rested my head on the pillow, holding his hand with both of mine. "If anyone comes in here," I said determinedly, "I'll tell them I'm sick, that you're helping me."

He pulled his hand from mine, then began to rub my face with both his hands, vigorously, as if to wake me.

"Calm down now," he said. "I will write you my address in Jaipur."

"What's your name?"

"John," he said. I did not ask him for his Indian name.

After a silence I asked, "Can you tell I'm sick?"

"All tourists get sick. Even I get sick when I return from Europe."

"Please open the window."

He hesitated. "The sand is blowing all over the cabin."

"I'm so hot," I said, almost panicking, "my breath is short."

He opened it. The desert invaded immediately. The sand slid across the table and gathered around the water bottles.

I asked him to take a water bottle and wet down the lungi I was stretched naked beneath.

"You don't want to waste your drinking water," he said.

"They're refilled with the water from the bathroom." I pointed to where he should start, the top of the lungi, just above my nipples.

He was nervous turning the bottle up, as though it held ink or blood. He poured lightly at first, thin streams that I felt stretch over the fabric, cooling my body down. He poured the water heavily over my crotch and thighs, then put his hand there and quickly withdrew it. When he had completely wet me down, he looked me over in sections, my chest, my stomach, torso, and legs. He looked closely, almost squinting, but didn't touch me again.

Finally, he said "You are dehydrated," rubbing two of his fingers over my lip. "I will get us chai."

He left the berth and came back with a large thermos. He poured out a cup and held it to my lips. It was too hot for tea, but I drank it for his effort.

He let himself stroke my hair and I closed my eyes, trusting him enough to fall asleep, leaving everything unlocked and unguarded.

I woke up some hours later. The sand had covered over everything. I could feel it on my cheeks like a stubble. I could feel it under my nails. It had gathered on the lungi between my legs, and between my fingers. John was gone. It seemed almost as easy to imagine he had never been with me. My possessions, becoming fewer and fewer, were untouched.

I looked out the window then, and in the darkness I was able to see the outline of homes just a few yards from the tracks, and people out on their doorsteps, the wind blowing their hair across their faces, and it must have been after midnight so it was strange to see them there, as though they'd roused themselves so not to miss our passing.

In the distance behind them I saw a sudden series of colorful lights flashing and rotating, a carnival a few miles from the tracks. That is how I realized this stop was not a small village, but perhaps our destination, Jaipur. I gathered my things in case the signs confirmed it when we pulled in. When I went to take the water bottle from the table, I found his address on a small, torn square of paper. Some of the ink had run under the ring left by the bottle. He wrote only his first name, John, and the number and street. Underneath he wrote Jaipur and underlined it. I slipped the paper in the front pocket of a pair of pants; then put them on.

The train moved slowly into the station as though it was dividing its way between the throngs of people. The crowds were taking refuge from the rains, the first in three years. I watched them with their umbrellas and sheets of newspaper over their heads, running from the rain but with expressions of excitement and joy. The rain affected them like a prophecy or a promise. I watched the others staring out at the rain as though it was a theater curtain.

People began to jump from the train and I watched them moving through the crowd until they were taken up and embraced by family, or took seats on the floor, waiting for the bicycle rickshaws to commence service, waiting for the rain to slow. I looked out over the crowd to see John but I didn't trust my memory of his face. I remembered the Star of Burma, and how he'd reached his hand out to show it.

I saw him then, pointing the way to a porter burdened with his bags. I left the train car, bag in tow, knocking into a woman and her child, and stepped out onto the platform where the crowds were swarming. He was lost somewhere, and when I gave up searching for him I was shocked by the part of me that had ventured out like a tentative root.

The rain that had entranced the crowd, falling heavily for a moment, stopped abruptly.

In the hotel I discovered a rash covering my side, like a continent mapped on a globe, and I felt nauseous looking at it, afraid to run my hand over it. Perhaps it was the fiber of the lungi, or the dye. My symptoms had improved since Banares, the vomiting had stopped. For two days, I could not leave the hotel. I watched to see if the rash would change, for it to get larger or disappear. I was feeling better, but now my body had this marking, and I could not reconcile it. There were moments when I could imagine wellness, but the long red patch remained. And only when I let myself stare at it and confront its otherness could I connect my mind to my body.

For two days I stayed in bed, giving myself pleasure by smoking cigarettes on my back and masturbating as often as I could. And this would go on through the night until the last guests would climb the gate and enter their rooms. It was impossible to sleep, thinking of the sickness and how far it would extend. It became a vigil, to watch the borders.

I believed that my sickness was the result of being inattentive. I scrutinized the rash throughout the nights, thinking my concentration could stem its advance. And it did, temporarily. On the second day in Jaipur, it seemed to have improved. Perhaps I had already grown used to it.

I stood up and pulled the kurta pajama over my head. It hung loosely, barely touching the rash. I think I did something silly then, like floating around the room waving the pajama pants in the air. I was delirious with life and with hunger. The Evergreen Hotel had a patio restaurant, always busy with travelers talking and playing chess. I sat at a large table where the talk was of Tiananmen Square. Many of them had been traveling in China when the protests began. They started talking about genocide and what it meant to be a casualty of a massive backlash, a massive intolerance. They all agreed that the ideal death would be one they choreographed themselves, that there was nothing more tragic than to be taken by history.

I ate voraciously; it was so seldom that I could hold food down. I'd kept my diet to glucose biscuits, bananas and curd. I couldn't help listening to them talk, though. It was like someone nearby whispering about you, lying.

A German sitting next to me asked my opinion.

"Nobody choreographs their own death," I said, shaking with stubbornness. "Not heroes and not cowards."

I kept thinking, everyone dies blindly. That's a reason to forgive them.

They moved the discussion to Israel, to the security cards that would be mandatory for Palestinians. People must have their integrity to survive, they agreed.

I took a rickshaw into the old city, the pink city, the walls around it cut from pink sandstone. Brightly painted suns crowned the lampposts. The streets were wider here, and for the first time in an Indian city I did not feel cramped. The rickshaw driver let me off at the Palace of the Winds, and I stood back from it so I could see its ornate edges and honeycombed windows. The women of an historical court were once kept here, and I could imagine their eyes flashing behind the filigreed bars on the windows.

Even walking away from it, I could feel the eyes of someone trained upon me. I walked aimlessly, browsing the book shops and stopping for juice at a fly-riddled stand. But when I stood up to walk again, my legs folded beneath me. I remembered drawing my hand back from the wheel of a rickshaw, a crowd forming over me, and silence my only answer to the questions in their eyes.

"How long have you been sick?"

"A couple of months, at least," I told the German. "Since I came to India."

"This is not normal," he said. "I've traveled India for three-and-a-half years and maybe I have been sick three weeks." He put ice in his napkin and told me to put it to my head.

"You must take advantage of the ice in India," he said lightly. "It is not easy to get."

An ugly swelled bruise came out on the side of my head where I'd fallen. I winced moving the ice across it.

"It looks painful," he said, "it's a wonder you got back here at all."

"I couldn't remember the name of the hotel. But when I said Evergreen, the rickshaw driver began laughing, calling it Nevergreen, and said he knew it well."

"Yes, well, they don't make commissions here."

"He charged twice the price," I said.

"Have you seen a doctor about that?" he asked, looking closely under the opened neck of my pajama.

I started to button it. “I don’t want to expose it to the sun.”

“It looks serious,” he said, “not to alarm you, but you should see someone about that.”

“I just need to get away, have a rest. I think it’s nerves. The cities are becoming too much for me. I should go somewhere quiet.”

“I’m leaving for Pushkar tomorrow. Why don’t you come?”

“No,” I said, “I’ve come to Jaipur to visit a friend.” I pulled the square of paper out of my money belt and tried to pronounce the street John had written, Chandi Ki Taksal.

The German took the paper from me. “I don’t see how you read this,” he said. “It looks like you put it through the wash.”

“How long will you stay in Pushkar?” I asked him. “Maybe I’ll see you there.”

“I don’t know,” he grinned, “I never know.”

The following morning I awoke before the sun came up. I stayed in bed with my eyes open, as if they were the only part of me awake. Through the screens on the windows, I could see the outline of trees and the empty chairs of the patio restaurant. It was completely still outside, as though my windows were actually frames around the stark images. If I could live like this, with just my eyes…

But I grew cold. The bed soaked through with sweat, a slight breeze through the window screen, unassuming as breath, passed over me like the hands of a lover.

The shower was cold, and I sat on the edge of my bed with the thin covers clutched around me. There were the first movements around the chairs outside my window from a group of newcomers with their baggage in tow. They sat and smoked cigarettes, waiting for the cooks to awaken.

I passed them as I was leaving. I smiled reservedly at the woman in the group, her hair cut like a pixie, a wistful, almost dreamy expression on her face. She said hello, turning the others' attention toward me. A man I'd seen her talking to turned to face me; a birthmark, like a cruel burn, covered half his face. I was startled when I saw him, and uneasy when I noticed he was smiling.

The sun was rising over the pink city, permeating and enriching its color. We passed through the gates and I already remembered these places, the fruit stands and bookshops, and it seemed for a moment that the city might be very small. The rickshaw driver was practically stoic as he drove, he was trying to convince me that he knew this address. He'd consulted with five other drivers, and I felt I had to keep asking just to keep him from pedaling to exhaustion. He swerved suddenly and took us down an unpaved side street that kept the rickshaw jumping and put an unbearable strain into his face. It was no surprise when at the first square we reached, he stopped pedaling and turned hesitantly toward me.

"We are here," he said.

"Where is here?" I asked with some amusement in my voice.

"The address you want to go."

"I see." I looked around and there were so many children and they were moving toward me with their hands already outstretched. I stepped out of the rickshaw and paid him the price we'd discussed.

"No, sir," I heard him say as the children took hold, "it is forty rupees."

They were shouting and pushing each other to shake my hand. Some of the young boys shook my hand elaborately or with such force I began to worry that they could overpower me. The girls were less secure in their interactions with me. The boys crowded them out. I pulled out the address for one of them who was eagerly asking, "Are you lost?"

He stared at the square of paper for some time, rubbing his thumb across it as the others looked on.

"English?" he asked finally.

I read the street name off the paper. The children just looked enthusiastic and confused. I put it away and started walking, losing some of them to their street games and to the ice-cream stands. The streets were dominated by the gem trade. Workers sat hovered over rotating wheels, refining gems at the end of their sticks. There were jewelry shops boasting custom work and silver. The men stood in their doorways, calling me in.

I would see him in a doorway, too, and my recognition would be immediate, and he would know by the way I hesitated to step any further that I had come for something impossible.

I did not see him though, and when I asked the other shopkeepers they did not know the street I tried to pronounce. I began to think he must have written this name to confuse them—when they said it to themselves their minds went blank.

I wanted to look into every doorway, see behind every curtain. The address he'd written was a hoax, a screen. But there was a part of me already resigned not to find him. I thought of us on that train—had we spoken at all? When I imagine us speaking now, there is a subtext of futility that drowns out our words.

I entered a shop. The man in the doorway offered chai. His expression was gentle and assuring as he put his arm around my shoulder. I realized that I wanted John to tell me I wasn't sick, no more than any other tourist, and that I wasn't alone. The man displayed a tray of rings.

I was looking at the stones. I was crying. The shopkeeper noticed at the same instant.

"It's just dust in my eye," I told him, and took the tissue he offered. I pointed to the center of the tray. "Is this a Star of Burma?" I asked.

"Very good," he said excitedly, "do you know how you can tell their value?" He didn't need to be a good salesman, but he was.

"Can't someone wire you the money from the States?" he asked, when I told him the price would break me.

"Yes, I can take your traveler's checks at a very good rate," he persisted.

I shuffled the last of my checks. This is another three months in India, I thought as I endorsed them. Somehow, I felt free of the burden of watching them diminish.

The white star is like a blossom trapped in the pink stone, like-something alive in a glass ball. You judge the value of the stone by the fullness of its star, by the spears of light it emits.

"You can sell this for hundreds of dollars back home," he said, but it fit my finger perfectly.

It was raining when I left his shop. I greeted it with the same enthusiasm I'd seen the Indians show at the train station. It was a brief rain, and there was a strange feeling of relief when it stopped. I came out of an alleyway to a large, paved street and hailed a rickshaw. The driver did not respond when I said Evergreen Hotel, but he began pedaling when I said Nevergreen. I thought of the name, and how it made the drivers laugh and I wondered if they'd ever thought it might apply to them, to their life in the desert, to its barrenness. Perhaps they only needed that light sprinkle of rain to assure them that all things come back.

And later, when the hotel guests sat laughing and talking around the tables as the sun sank behind the carnival lights, I wondered how they drew their strength and where their laughter came from. I wondered if they didn't cling to their separateness, to the fact that they were tourists. And maybe it is better to travel with a camera, to consign those needy faces to paper, or to write letters, taking control over each story as you retell it. Even a distant observer of India could believe he had the power to save her people from anonymity, from their numbers. A photo makes them the object of someone's love, and they will carefully assemble themselves before the camera as though it was a wedding picture, their marriage to you—just for looking at them.

I could hear the crickets, and the waiters squatting in a row, singing to themselves as they washed the plates in large tubs. The sun had set and many of the tourists had dispersed, either to their rooms or out for the evening. I did not want to go to my room. It meant looking at myself in the mirror, taking off my clothes and counting the ribs and notches of spine. And there were sweet flowers outside that enabled me to forget the smell of my body. When I looked at my face in a mirror, I saw the face of a beggar, the white paste on my lips from dehydration, the skull that seemed to be rubbing out the skin. In my eyes, I saw the remoteness of my lover's eyes.

A plate fell from a waiter's hands and shattered. The last tourists laughed and applauded. But soon afterward, they gathered their things and went inside.

In my room, I rolled my clothes into my suitcase. I went through my money belt. It scared me then—when I realized how little money I had left. It was as though I had put a pressure on myself to expire before it did. I almost hoped that I would, so I would not have to depend on mercy.

5.

The busride to Pushkar brought on a fever that ravaged me for a week. The bus was cramped with people. The seats were filled with mothers and infants. I pushed my way to the back of the bus and leaned against a rusted exit door. We were jostled back and forth over the unpaved roads that wound their way up the desert mountains. The people stood very close and still, shielding their eyes from the sand blowing in the windows and the brightness of the sun, which bleached out the landscape. The exhaust fumes were coming up from the floor of the bus and I became drowsy and short of breath. I'd catch myself sleeping while holding myself upright. I was struggling to keep my eyes open. I wasn't sure if I was dreaming the faces gathered around me, the Indian faces watching and laughing. I let my knees slacken and fell almost instantly asleep on my bag. But I soon felt them nudging me awake, shouting over the space I was taking up. They pulled me to my feet and were laughing again. I stood there with my head toppled forward like a puppet for their amusement.

By the time we reached Pushkar, I had vomited out a back window and had begun feeling the dizzy signs of fever. I felt shame amongst the others and kept my arm crossed over my face. When the bus pulled in, I waited for the others to gather their bags and leave the bus before I began to drag my own bag behind me.

A young boy approached me. I was standing still at the center of the activity. The driver was distributing the baggage alongside the bus, and the vendors wove their way through the new arrivals with food and strung flowers hanging from their arms. The boy offered to take the bag for me.

"I will take you to my uncle's lodge," he said. He was wearing the customary earrings of the Rajasthani villagers, six-petaled flowers with rubies, sapphires, or diamonds on each petal. The men wear them in both ears, and it seems to make them all soft around the eyes. His long, black eyelashes made him look both feminine and sad. We walked silently together. There are no rickshaws in Pushkar, and the road was quiet and untraveled.

Pushkar is a small village, a ring of civilization around a lake. The lake is holy; it is claimed to be the footprint of Brahma, and the businesses around it have sprung up like mushrooms. But the businesses are seasonal operations and haven't destroyed the lake as a place of prayer and worship. There is an almost hypnotic rippling on the surface of the lake, a calm that manifests itself in the pace of life around it.

We arrived at the Lotus Lodge, a small establishment of maybe eight rooms and a courtyard which sloped down to the lakefront. The boy dropped my bag and called out to the owner who approached me with his hand extended. He shook mine enthusiastically and asked the boy to make chai.

We sat at a table on the lawn and he pulled his accounting book from under his arm. His name was Acharya. He was balding at the top of his head and wore wire-framed glasses, which acted as his business attire. The only clothing he wore was a pair of underwear cut like shorts and the Brahmin chord, a janai, loosely hanging from his shoulder like a sash.

He told me the room would be very inexpensive because there was no business here in the summer.

"Why haven't you gone with your friends to Kashmir?" he asked.

"I'm traveling alone," I told him. "I wanted to come someplace quiet."

He began at once writing in his book and simultaneously telling me of the difficulties he'd had in getting someone to fix the fans in the room. While he talked, I looked over at the storage room, in which the boy was squatting before the fire, making our chai. There was no light on inside and it seemed like a cave in there, the boy's eyes like an animal's.

Acharya explained that the room would be ten rupees a night since the fan was out and I'd most likely prefer to bring my cot out on the lawn and sleep there.

"Then you have only to worry about the monkeys in the morning," he said. "When they come down from the trees they like to run along this back wall." Even then, a family of monkeys was playing on it. "The boy did the painting on it," he continued. "It is the symbol of the Om."

Just then, the boy emerged with a tray and the two cups of chai. He bowed with a strange formality as he served it to us, and his uncle asked him then to fill the shower tanks with lake water. Acharya and I sipped our tea in the heat, watching the boy trudge with the water buckets from the lake to the top of the hill where a cement shower room was built for guests.

By the time we had taken our chai, I was ready to lie down, and the boy walked me to a room and placed my bag inside. I stretched out on my cot and closed my eyes, and the boy started singing one of the popular Indian songs I'd heard reproduced in every wedding procession and played in the streets from every radio. He sang it very quietly as he began to sweep the corners of the room.

The fever escalated rapidly, as it so often did. There was always the exhaustion, but the fever didn't allow sleep. My mind was moving restlessly like a fly. The delirium is often sensual; the whole body remembers.

My fingers on the porch screen; a memory surfaces with the heat and chill of fever. A man my father had employed to cut down a diseased tree that grew in our backyard. I was very young then, but I remember his features, a skinny laborer with moles on his neck and shoulders, some self-performed tattoos on his arms and chest that had faded and looked more like bruises or natural markings. I watched from the screen porch. The man, every now and then, would look over his shoulder and wink.

When the tree fell, the man ran his hand over the wet, open trunk.

"Wanna look at this, kid?" he asked. I went out and stood beside him. His sweat smelled like chicken soup. He pointed out the maggots spawning in the tree's center. The trunk was soft and stank like garbage. "Imagine living in that," the man commented. "Now stand back."

The tar emerged with slow, thorough, suffocating precision. The man rubbed his hands on his jeans, the smoke rising up before his face. "Pity we couldn't have yanked out the whole thing." He pointed at the roots running under the porch, thick as pipes.

Then the fever felt like fingers on my throat, and I was gasping. The boy was sitting with me then, and by his bare feet he had a pail of lake water, and using an old rag, he wet me down with it. He did it with patience, as though tending to me was all he had to do for the day, and he continued singing, a melody that wove its way in and out of my delirium.

And he did this for days that I could not keep track of—keeping me in the shade during the day, and carrying first my cot and then me out to the lawn at night, where it was cooler. He fed me curd and bananas in the afternoon, dahl at night. Finally the fever broke, and he quickly took the bedding from my room to wash.

At sundown, I left the room and sat weakly in a chair facing the lake. The sky was divided—a band of fiery orange and, just above it, a night sky, black and heavy with stars. There was no one on the lawn, just the long shadows of the trees from behind me. There was a cool breeze coming off the desert, and the patches of grass felt cool on my bare feet. This is how I will die, I thought, just after the pain breaks, and I can feel again.

I sat there silently until Acharya drew up a chair beside me. "You feel better?" he asked.

"Yes," I said. "And thank the boy. He was a great comfort."

"He is a hard worker, I was lucky to have found him. He was very sick when I first saw him. It cost me a great deal to have him taken care of."

"You are his uncle?" I asked.

"I suppose so," he laughed. "He is convinced of it."

"He must be grateful to you."

"Yes," he said. "I let him live here. He cooks and cleans. He is quiet."

Just then, I heard some music, faint but beautiful, which made our shadows on the lawn and the surface of the lake seem as luxurious as life depicted in a miniature painting.

"That's him," he said. "He is a good musician. All of his family played."

I remembered the melody. He had been humming it at my bedside. I looked over my shoulder and there was a fire burning in the storage room, and in that light the boy was playing.

"Both of his parents died. They were villagers, musicians. His father died when he was young. His mother died slowly; she was very sick. She could not see; she could not walk. He would come miles by foot to Pushkar to play the instrument his father left him. He would make money and bring back food and medicine to her. He was always playing, and he was always serious. Then one day he came out of the desert. I noticed him, from far off. He looked so broken and so old, like a sadhu. But he was just a boy, crying over the loss of his mother. I could see he was very sick himself. I told him he could work for me when he got well. He has worked for me for five years."

He turned toward the storage room where I was watching the boy's shadow flicker along the wall, and shouted out for chai. The boy put his instrument down and went for glasses.

Acharya leaned toward me from his chair. "I have alcohol," he whispered, "the boy picks it up for me in Ajmer. Pushkar is dry. It is not acceptable for a Brahmin to drink." I could smell the liquor on him then and his eyes were deep with his confession. "That makes me an unacceptable Brahmin."

The boy came with chai in tall glasses. He handed us each a glass, and smiled at me as though he were pleased with his nursing and my recovery. He said goodnight and walked back to the room where the fire was burning. I saw him take his lungi off and spread it on the floor, and that is where he slept.

Acharya spiked his tea with whiskey he had transferred to a plastic water bottle. "The inspectors come whenever they want," he said. "They come to look for drugs in the rooms. They look over everything. It would be a disgrace for me to have alcohol found here. They would ask for baksheesh, more than I could pay."

"Have you had any trouble in the past?" I asked.

"No problems yet," he said. "But they came at night once, and I had been drinking and the boy had to talk to them for me. He told them I was sick."

He pulled his legs up to his chest and sat rocking for a while, like a child, but with a troubled face.

"He was so happy after they'd gone. I felt relieved but not happy. I felt ashamed of myself for having involved him. I could not accept his help, even though I had pulled him out of the desert."

In the morning I awoke to the shrill cries of peacocks, hysterical in the trees, as though they were stranded there. Acharya was still sleeping, in a cot near mine.

I walked down to the lake. There were groups of monkeys huddled by its shore, and a swimmer at its center. I took off my shirt and pants and left them in a pile at the edge of the lawn. I walked down to the water and put my foot into it, and watched it, blurry under the surface. I worried that someone would take notice of my illness, which seemed to afflict my whole body in one way or another. I had the ravaged look of a holocaust survivor. The patch on my chest had grown, and there were other small, irregular marks on my legs and thighs.

The swimmer had made his way back to the shore, and was only a few yards away before I recognized him as the boy who'd taken me here and nursed me. He began to call for me, waving his hands above his head.

"The water is good for you," he said, laughing. "Don't be afraid."

I stepped carefully into the water, then pushed myself away from the edge using my feet on the algae-covered rocks. He swam toward me and grasped my hand when he could reach it. We kept ourselves afloat with just our legs paddling in the currents beneath us. He put his hands on my shoulders.

"Try to stay still," he said. He was smiling and drawing me close to him.

"What's that?" I asked, almost jumping out of the water.

"That's the fish," he laughed. "They're kissing us."

It felt suddenly like there were hundreds of them, brushing between our legs, lightly connecting their mouths to us.

"I should go back," I said.

"I'll go with you." He offered his hand again and we swam back together. He pulled me up on shore and carried my clothing down to me.

"Do you want chai?" he asked.

"No," I said. "Today I am going to walk and see the rest of Pushkar."

"Let me take you?"

"Yes," I said, "you can be my guide."

He was wearing Rajasthani shoes that point at the toe, his lungi and turban with multiple knots and gatherings. He carried his instrument with him. The shops were quiet. The tailors sat on their folded fabrics smoking bidis and reading newspapers. Cows wandered through the streets with flowers in their mouths. When we passed a tourist, he lifted his instrument to his chest the way country musicians in America hold their violins. And he started to play, something that repeated itself, with the bells dangling on the bow keeping time. It was a sad, serial melody that developed slowly and slightly, music that is sweet and painful, returning mournfully to its themes like a memory of childhood. There is even a resonance to pain—a nostalgia—that makes it hard to die.

He kept his eyes averted as he played; he wanted the music to ask for coins. He wanted to slip behind his sorrowful invocation, invisible. He wanted the music and not his eyes to make the listener sympathetic.

The woman he played for stopped and watched him, then handed him a five rupee note. When she had walked off, he continued playing for me, and even as he looked at me, his eyes were following the music.

We sat down in a restaurant boasting pizza. "The prices are too high here," he said.

"I'll buy," I said. I was already out of breath.

When the food arrived, I couldn't eat. I was sweating heavily. Suddenly, my circumstances terrified me. I would barely be able to afford another week here before the money ran out, and there was perhaps less time than that before my health would fail me entirely.

I sat there squeezing my head in my hands, trying to stop the anxious thoughts. But I couldn't stop them. I could not accept the arrangements I had made for myself. I had cornered myself: I had to die or beg for charity. But I couldn't beg.

The boy asked me, "Are you going to be sick?"

"Yes," I told him, and I put my hands over my eyes so that he wouldn't see me crying.

"What's wrong with you?" he asked.

"I'm tired. My resistance is down."

"We will go back now," he said, standing.

He took up his instrument and walked a few paces behind me, playing. It seemed as though I was walking through my own funeral procession, with people turning their heads as we walked. The desert whistling behind the awninged shops made the whole town seem like a painted curtain. He followed me halfway around the lake before I turned to him and asked his name.

"Sanjay," he said.

Someone called out from a chai shop and I turned around. It was the German I'd met in Jaipur. I walked back to see him. He was sitting in a large wicker chair, smiling.

"It's good to see you here. The last time I saw you, you were telling me how much you needed a rest. It's restful here, though I can't say you look any better for it."

"It's worse," I said, joining him at the table.

Sanjay sat down, too, but looked uncomfortable and kept his attention on the street. Eventually, another musician boy, a little older than him, approached. They spoke to each other, often glancing back at the German and myself, until I asked Sanjay to go on without me.

He looked sadly at me, but didn't question the suggestion. He gathered his instrument and bow, and asked if I would see him later. I assured him I would, and he and his friend walked off.

"Have you seen a doctor, yet?" the German asked.

"No, I don't have the money for it."

"There's a public hospital in Jodhpur, just across the street from the train station."

"I don't need a hospital. The boy is taking care of me."

"He's lovely," the German said, winking, "How long have you had him?"

"A few days. He helped me through a fever."

"What kind of medicine is he treating you with? Are you in pain?"

"No medicine, just cold rags and simple food."

"If you're in pain I can help you," he said. "I have an opium connection here."

"I don't know," I said. "I had a problem with heroin before, and I don't have any money."

"That's OK," he said. "You'll feel rich."

He offered to bring it by the Lotus Lodge later that evening.

"I'll have to leave India," he confided. "My permit ran out years ago. I read tarot cards to make a living. Tourists sometimes pay me in American money. I tell them my story and most of them are horrified by the idea of being trapped in India, and they sympathize with me. But I've loved India. It changes you. In Hamburg, my goal was to work in a bank, or to sell good German cars. In India, I'd be content to have a group of young boys who would follow me out into the desert like a holy man." He laughed and looked over his shoulder as though he expected the desert to present him with a mirage, a preview of his enlightenment. "They'll catch up with me soon," he said, growing more serious. "Otherwise, I'm afraid if I do stay in India, I'll be tempted to walk out into the desert, even if I can't find anybody foolish enough to follow me. It sounds crazy, but it's a fantasy of mine."

It was late afternoon when I left the chai house. Sanjay was waiting on the street. He hesitated, though, until I called him over. Then he quickly took my arm and asked me if I would write my name on the face of his instrument.

"Write it under that tree," he said, pointing.

It was a beautiful spot he had chosen. We sat in the shade and he handed the instrument over to me. I took out my pen and scratched my name over the bleached, leather face. My markings were tentative. He watched over my shoulder and I could hear the anticipation in his breathing. I felt at first I was defacing the beautiful instrument which had four taut strings running along the wooden neck and over the gourdlike body, but he squeezed my arm to encourage me further. I thought it strange that he might remember me, sitting there and writing under that tree, by some markings he could not read.

We stretched out under the tree. He laid on his back with the instrument on his chest, plucking the strings with his long fingernails. He inclined his head so that it almost touched my chest. His eyes were closed and he was smiling.

"What are you thinking about?" I asked him.

"My mother let me play for her like this. When my father died, she wanted to die, too. There was no rain and we lost everything. Then she got very sick and she stopped eating. Every meal I would force her to eat. She stopped being able to see, and then she said that she was already dead and she told me to go to Pushkar and not to come back. But I went back anyway," he laughed, nodding his head, "and I would play for her because it reminded her of my father. Then before she died she asked me to play the song I was just playing for you, and she started to sing, only quietly, but like she did when there was food to cook, and friends still in the village."

I was trembling at his closeness. I wanted to lie beside him for the rest of the day, but there was only a short time to enjoy him. His friend approached and stood over us, laughing, then took his bow and began jabbing at Sanjay with it. He stood up and they began arguing.

Finally, Sanjay said the other boy wanted to play for me. He stood silently by the tree. I couldn't understand his expression, whether he felt ashamed of his friend, of me, or of himself. But his friend started to play and tapped his foot as he did. And it was the same melody I'd heard Sanjay play, but with none of the sadness, with a strange mockery instead. And when he finished playing, he reached his hand out to me.

"You don't play as well as him," I said, looking over at Sanjay's quiet face. Then I stood up to go.

Sanjay walked beside me, apologizing. I told him it didn't matter, that I was tired and wanted to nap.

"I'm going to help you get better," he said.

I grasped his arm with a strength that surprised me. "You're not going to make me well," I said. "I'm dying and you're not going to make me well."

He pulled his arm from my hand and ran off.

By the time I arrived back, I had cramps so severe I couldn't stand straight. I went into the shower room, took off my clothes and let the water run. I stretched out on the floor beneath it. I felt something warm on my leg and it was clotted blood running from my rectum. I wanted to scream but put my hand in my mouth and bit it. I watched the blood disperse in the water and didn't move until the water tank had emptied, and I was shivering. The blood seemed to have stopped but the pains were sharp. I sat on the shower floor, my teeth chattering, praying for the German to come with the opium—indirectly, it was the first time I'd prayed for medicine.

It was Sanjay who found me, though, and put my arm around his neck, holding me up and carrying me along to the room. He looked astonished over my condition, as though nothing had led up to it, as though he'd never seen me sick before.

"You should go to the hospital," he said. His eyes were sadder than usual. I imagined him thinking, Because you won't let me make you well.

At that moment I wanted to tell him to try, that I would try also, but it was too unfair to do that to him again. His mother had waited too long before she sang with him. Even if I wanted to, I couldn't remember that tune.

"My medicine is coming," I said. "My friend will be here soon."

He woke me when the German finally came.

"Thomas," I said, already delirious with fever, "I can't believe you're here."

"This is Heinz," he said, taking my hand. "I don't know if I should give you this."

"Give it to me," I said. "It's like morphine, right? That's what they give soldiers when they can't help them."

He nervously paced the room and asked Sanjay to bring us chai. "I'll mix it in your tea. Drink it fast, it's bitter."

Sanjay brought the tea and hesitantly left the room when the German asked him to.

The opium affected me powerfully, but not in the way we'd hoped. It stunned me. I threw up. I was nauseous with the slightest movement, and sat still at the edge of thc cot.

"Hospital," was all I said, gasping for breath.

The German paced nervously. I was throwing up in a bucket by the side of the cot, and the smell was pungent, already like a hospital. I think he smelled death on me and that propelled him to action. It wouldn't be easy getting me to Jodhpur, and I knew he was worried that I wouldn't make it. How would he ever explain himself to the authorities, traveling with a long-expired visa and a dead American?

Under the influence of the opium, I didn't make much sense. I remember Sanjay coming into the room and taking out the bucket, and touching my face with his hands. I twisted the ring from my finger, then, and put it in his hand. He was crying when the German finished packing my bag and led me away.

6.

I saw an omen in the streets of Jodhpur. In front of a store I saw a white horse staggering on a mound of trash. It was tied to a post with a tethered rope around its neck. Its front leg looked broken but it was made to stand by the short length of rope, and it seemed to have been in this condition for some time. Something like gangrene had set in and the horse's flesh was putrid.

I was wheeled into the emergency ward of Mahatma Gandhi Public Hospital. They pressed me to lie down on a rusty stretcher with rubber wheels. The wheels squealed and turned off in odd directions so that the short, nervous intern who was guiding me through the hospital corridors had to run along the sides of it to save us from hitting a wall or one of the many spectators.

I was wheeled into a room where a woman and her daughter were standing. The little girl was weeping, her face pressed into the hot pink fabric of her mother's sari. Behind a green curtain, a man was screaming and crying.

They cleaned me up, brought me into the ward, and put me on an IV for dehydration and malnutrition. The German saw me settled in, a crowd of interns gathered by my bedside, prodding me.

"I apologize," he said. "I can't stay with you. The hospital will drive me crazy."

"So will the desert," I told him.

"Get well," he said, "and come back to Pushkar."

In the bed near mine, an old man from a village not far from Jodhpur was connected to tubes. The men of the village had been sleeping on mats around his bed since he'd arrived. Old world loyalty. They'd marveled at the beeping and pumping machines that kept the old man breathing, but an American was even more interesting. They spoke no English but gathered around my bed, smiling and bowing and excitedly talking amongst themselves.

The villagers are trying their turbans on my head, one by one. The fever sweeps over me. I no longer make any sense to them.

"Thomas, let me play," I say, and the villagers find a place for me at the card table. An intern pushes them aside impatiently. The IV has caused a rash. It feels like worms under my skin.

One of the sisters is crying at the bedside. Sanjay squeezes out a cloth and puts it on my forehead. I know his song, now, and I hear my voice intoning it. The villagers stand at the foot of the bed. They look like a hundred grandfathers. They're patient with me. I keep looking back; I keep stumbling at the start of the desert.